S0-BIM-239

God's Little Acre

God's Little Acre

by

Erskine Caldwell

NAL

NEW AMERICAN LIBRARY

TIMES MIRROR

NEW YORK

DISTRIBUTED BY W. W. NORTON & COMPANY, INC.

Published by The New American Library, Inc.
1301 Avenue of the Americas, New York, New York 10019

Distributed by W. W. Norton & Company, Inc.
500 5th Avenue, New York, New York 10036

Reissued by The New American Library, Inc. 1976

Printed in the United States of America

1   2   3   4   5   6   7   8   9   0

Chapter I

SEVERAL YARDS OF undermined sand and clay broke loose up near the top, and the land slid down to the floor of the crater. Ty Ty Walden was so angry about the landslide that he just stood there with the pick in his hands, knee-deep in the reddish earth, and swore about everything he could think of. The boys were ready to stop work, anyway. It was mid-afternoon then, and they had been down in the ground digging in the big hole since daylight that morning.

"Why in the pluperfect hell did that dirt have to break loose up there just when we were getting deep?" Ty Ty said, glaring at Shaw and Buck. "Now ain't that something!"

Before either of them could answer their father, Ty Ty clutched the pick handle in both hands and hurled it with all his might against the side of the crater. He let it go at that. There were times, though, when he was so provoked that he would pick up a stick and flail the ground with it until he dropped exhausted.

Buck gripped his knees with his hands and pulled his legs out of the loose earth and sat down to shake the sand and gravel out of his shoes. He was thinking of that great mass of earth they would have to shovel and carry out of the hole before they could begin digging again.

"It's time we were starting a new hole," Shaw told his father. "We've been digging in this one for about two months already, and we ain't struck nothing yet but a lot of hard work. I'm tired of this hole. We can't get anything out of this one, no matter how much deeper we dig."

Ty Ty sat down and fanned his hot face with his hat. There was no fresh air down in the big hole, and the crater was hotter than a pail of barbecue hash.

"The trouble with you boys is that you ain't found the patience that I've got," he said, fanning and wiping his face. "I've been digging in this land close on to fifteen years now, and I'm aiming to dig here fifteen more, if need be. But I've got a feeling the need won't be. I figure we're going to strike pay pretty soon. I feel it in my bones these hot days. We can't stop and start all over again every time a little loose dirt breaks away from the rim up there and comes sliding down. Wouldn't

5

be no sense in starting a new hole all over again every time that happened. We've just got to keep plugging away like nothing ever happened. That's the only way to do it. You boys are too impatient about little things."

"Impatient, hell!" Buck said, spitting into the red clay. "We don't need patience—what we need is a diviner. Looks like you would know better than to dig without one."

"There you go again talking like the darkies, son," Ty Ty said resignedly. "I wish you had the sense not to listen to what the darkies say. That ain't a thing in the world but superstition. Now take me, here. I'm scientific. To listen to the darkies talk, a man would believe they have got more sense than I have. All they know about it is that talk about diviners and conjurs."

Shaw picked up his shovel and started climbing to the top of the ground.

"Well, I'm quitting for the day, anyway," Shaw said. "I want to go to town tonight."

"Always quitting work in the middle of the day to get ready to go to town," Ty Ty said. "You'll never get rich doing that. All you do when you go to town is to hang around the poolroom a while and then go chasing after some woman. If you'd stay at home, we'd get somewhere."

Shaw got down on his hands and knees when he got halfway to the top and crawled the rest of the way to keep from slipping backward. They watched him go up the side of the crater and stand on the ground above.

"Who does he go to see in town so often?" Ty Ty asked his other son. "He'll be getting into trouble if he don't watch out. Shaw ain't used to women yet. They can do him dirty and he won't know about it till it's too late to stop the clock."

Buck sat on the other side of the hole from his father and crumbled the dry clay in his fingers.

"I don't know," he said. "Nobody in particular. He's got a new girl every time I hear about it. He likes anything with skirts on."

"Why in the pluperfect hell can't he let the women alone? There ain't no sense in a man going rutting every day in the whole year. The women will wear Shaw to a frazzle. When I was a young fellow, I never carried on like he does about the women. What's got into him, anyway? He ought to be satisfied just to sit at home and look at the girls in the house."

"Don't ask me. I don't care what he does in town."

Shaw had been out of sight for several minutes, but suddenly he appeared up above and called down to Ty Ty. They saw Shaw with surprise.

"What's the matter, son?" Ty Ty asked.

"There's a man coming across the field, Pa," he said. "He's coming from the house."

Ty Ty stood up, looking around in all directions as though he could see over the top of the hole twenty feet above.

"Who is he, son? What does he want out here?"

"I can't make out who he is yet," Shaw said. "But it looks like somebody from town. He's all dressed up."

Buck and his father gathered up the picks and shovels and climbed out of the crater.

When they reached the top of the ground, they saw a large fat man walking laboriously over the rough field towards them. He was coming slowly in the heat, and his pale blue shirt was plastered to his chest and stomach with perspiration. He stumbled helplessly over the rough ground, unable to look down and see his feet.

Ty Ty raised his hand and waved.

"Why, that's Pluto Swint," he said. "Reckon what Pluto wants out here?"

"I couldn't recognize Pluto all dressed up like that," Shaw said. "I wouldn't have known him at all."

"Looking for something for nothing," Buck replied to his father. "That's all he ever does, that I've heard about."

Pluto came closer, and they went over to the shade of the live-oak tree and sat down.

"Hot weather. Ty Ty," Pluto said, stumbling over the ground. "Hello there, boys. How are you folks making out, Ty Ty? You ought to build a road out here to the holes so I could drive my car on it. You ain't quitting for the day, are you?"

"You ought to stay in town and wait for the cool of the evening before coming out here, Pluto," Ty Ty said.

"I wanted to drive out and see you folks."

"Ain't it hot, though?"

"Reckon I can stand it, if anybody can. How are you folks making out?"

"Ain't complaining," Ty Ty said.

Pluto sat down against the trunk of the live-oak tree and panted like a dog running rabbits in mid-summer. The perspiration oozed from the flat flesh on his face and neck, and trickled down upon his pale blue shirt, turning it several shades darker. He sat there for a while, too tired and hot to move or to speak.

Buck and Shaw rolled cigarettes and lit them.

"So you ain't complaining," Pluto said. "Well, that's something to be thankful for. I reckon there's enough to complain about these days if a fellow wants to bellyache some. Cotton ain't worth the raising no longer, and the darkies eat the watermelons as fast as they ripen on the vines. There's not much sense in trying to grow things for a living these days. I never was much of a farmer, anyway."

Pluto stretched out and put his arms under his head. He was becoming more comfortable in the shade.

"Strike anything lately?" he asked.

"Nothing much," Ty Ty said. "The boys are after me to start a new hole, but I ain't decided yet, We've gone about twenty feet in that one, and the sides are starting to cave in. I reckon we might just as well go and dig somewhere else for a spell. A new one won't be any worse than an old one."

"What you folks need is an albino to help you out," Pluto said. "They tell me that a man ain't got as much of a chance as a snowball in hell without an albino to help."

Ty Ty sat up and looked at Pluto.

"A what, Pluto?"

"An albino."

"What in the pluperfect hell is an albino, Pluto? I never heard of one before. Where'd you hear of it?"

"You know what I'm talking about. You know you've heard about them."

"It's slipped my mind completely, if I have, then."

"He's one of these all-white men who look like they are made out of chalk or something just as white. An albino is one of these all-white men, Ty Ty. They're all white; hair and eyes and all, they say."

"Oh, that," Ty Ty said, sitting back again. "I didn't recognize what you were talking about at first. Sure I know what one of those is. I've heard the darkies talking about it, but I don't pay no attention to what the colored people say. I reckon I could use one though, if I knew where to find it. Never saw one of the creatures in my whole life."

"You folks need one here."

"I always said I'd never go in for none of this superstition and conjur stuff, Pluto, but I've been thinking all the time that one of those albinoes is what we need. You understand, though, I'm scientific all the way through. I wouldn't have anything to do with conjur. That's one thing in the world I ain't going to fool with. I'd heap rather sleep in the bed with a rattler than monkey around with conjur."

"A fellow was telling me he saw one the other day," Pluto said. "And that's a fact."

"Where?" Ty Ty asked, jumping to his feet. "Where'd he see it, Pluto? Somewhere around here, Pluto?"

"Down in the lower end of the county somewhere. He wasn't far away. You could go and get him and be back here with him inside of ten or twelve hours at the most. I don't reckon you'd have any trouble catching him, but it wouldn't do any harm to tie him up a little before starting back. He lives in the swamp, and he might not like the feel of solid ground."

Shaw and Buck moved closer to the tree where Pluto was sitting.

"A real honest-to-God albino?" Shaw asked.

"As real as the day is long."

"Alive and walking around?"

"That's what the fellow told me," Pluto answered. "And that's a fact."

"Where is he now?" Buck asked. "Reckon we could catch him easy?"

"I don't know how easy you folks can catch him, because it might take a powerful lot of persuading to get him to come up here on solid ground. But then, I reckon you folks know how to go about getting him."

"We'll rope him," Buck said.

"I didn't aim to say as much, but I reckon you folks caught on to what I had in mind. I don't go around recommending the breaking of laws as a rule, and when I hint at it, I expect folks to leave me out of it."

"How big is he?" Shaw asked.

"The fellow didn't recall."

"Big enough to do some good, I hope," Ty Ty said.

"Oh, sure. It's not the size that counts, anyway. It's the all-whiteness, Ty Ty."

"What's his name?"

"The fellow didn't recall," Pluto said. "And that's a fact."

Ty Ty broke off a double-sized chew of tobacco and hitched up his suspenders. He began walking up and down in the shade, looking at nothing save the ground at his feet. He was too excited to sit still any longer.

"Boys," he said, still walking up and down in front of them, "the gold-fever has got me steaming again. Go to the house and fix up the automobile for a trip. Make sure that all the tires are pumped up hard and tight, and put plenty of water in the radiator. We're going to take a trip right off."

"After the albino, Pa?" Buck said.

"You're durn tooting, son," he said, walking faster. "We're going to get that all-white man if I have to bust a gut getting there. But there's not going to be any of this conjur hocus-pocus mixed up in it. We're going about this business scientifically."

Buck started towards the house at once, but Shaw turned and came back.

"What about the rations for those darkies, Pa?" he asked. "Black Sam said at dinner-time that he's all out of meat and corn meal at his house, and Uncle Felix said he didn't have anything at his house this morning to eat for breakfast. They told me to be sure and say something to you about it so they could have something to eat for supper tonight. They both looked a little hollow-eyed to me."

"Now, son, you know good and well I ain't got the time to be worrying about darkies eating," Ty Ty said. "What in the pluperfect hell do you mean by bothering me right when I'm the busiest, and getting ready to go after that all-white man? We've got to get down to the swamps and catch that albino before he gets away. You tell Black Sam and Uncle Felix that I'll try to fix them up with something to cook just as soon as we find that albino and bring him back."

Shaw still did not leave. He waited for several minutes, glancing at his father.

"Black Sam said he was going to butcher that mule he's plowing and eat him, if you don't give him some rations soon. He showed me his belly this morning. It's flat under his ribs."

"You go tell Black Sam that if he kills that mule and eats him, I'll take out after him and run his ass ragged before I quit. I ain't going to have darkies worrying me about rations at a time like this. You tell Black Sam to shut his mouth and leave that old mule alone and plow that cotton out there."

"I'll tell him," Shaw said, "but he's liable to eat the mule, anyway. He said he was so hungry he didn't know what he might take a notion to do next."

"You go tell him what I said, and I'll attend to him after we finish roping this albino."

Shaw shrugged his shoulders and started for the house behind Buck.

Across the field the two Negro men were plowing in the newground. There was very little land remaining under cultivation on the farm then. Fifteen or twenty acres of the place had been potted with holes that were anywhere from ten to thirty feet deep, and twice as wide. The newground had been cleared that spring to raise cotton on, and there was about twenty-five acres of it. Otherwise, there would not have been sufficient land that year for the two share-croppers to work. Year by year the area of cultivated land had diminished as the big holes in the ground increased. By that fall, they would probably have to begin digging in the newground, or else close to the house.

Pluto cut off a fresh chew of tobacco from the long yellow plug he carried in his hip pocket.

"How do you folks know there's gold in the ground, Ty Ty?" he asked. "You folks have been digging around here for the past fifteen years now, and you ain't struck a lode yet, have you?"

"It won't be long now, Pluto. With that all-white man to divine it, it's going to turn up for sure. I feel it in my bones right now."

"But how do you know there's gold in the ground on this farm? You've been digging here since 'way back yonder, and you ain't struck it yet. Everybody between here and the Savannah River talks about finding gold, but I ain't seen none of it."

"You're just hard to convince, Pluto."

"I ain't seen it," Pluto said. "And that's a fact."

"Well, I ain't exactly struck a lode yet," Ty Ty said, "but we're getting pretty durn near to it. I feel it in my bones that we're getting warm. My daddy told me there was gold on this land, and nearly everybody else in Georgia has told me so, and only last Christmas the boys dug up a nugget that was as big as a guinea egg. That proves to my satisfaction that there's gold under the ground, and I aim to get it out before I die. I ain't aiming to give up looking for it yet. If we can find that albino and rope him, I know good and well we're going to strike the lode. The darkies dig for gold all the time, all over the whole country, even up there in Augusta, I hear, and that's a pretty good sign there's gold somewhere."

Pluto screwed up his mouth and spat a stream of golden-yellow tobacco juice at a lizard under a rotten limb ten feet away. His aim was perfect. The scarlet lizard darted out of sight with his eyes stinging from Pluto's tobacco juice.

Chapter II

"I DON'T KNOW," Pluto said, looking over the tops of his shoes for some other object at which to spit tobacco juice. "I don't know. Somehow it seems to me like a waste of time to go digging these great big holes in the ground looking for gold. Maybe I'm just lazy, though. If I had the gold-fever like you folks, I reckon I'd be tearing up the patch like the rest. Somehow the gold-fever don't seem to cling to me like it does to you folks. I can throw it off just by sitting down and thinking about it some."

"When you get the real honest-to-goodness gold-fever, Pluto, you can't shake it loose to save your soul. Maybe you ought to be glad you ain't got the fever. I don't regret it none myself, now that it's in my blood, but I reckon I ain't like you. A man can't be lazy and have the fever at the same time. It makes a man be up and doing."

"I haven't got the time to spend digging in the ground," Pluto said. "I just can't spare it."

"If you had the fever, you wouldn't have time for nothing else," Ty Ty said. "It gets a man just like liquor does, or chasing women. When you get a taste for it, you ain't going to sit still till you get it some more. It just keeps up like that, adding up all the time."

"I reckon I understand it a little better now," Pluto said. "But I still ain't got it."

"I don't reckon you'll be apt to get it, either, till you train down so you can work some."

"My size don't hinder me. It gets in my way sometimes, but I get around that."

Pluto spat haphazardly to the left. The lizard had not come back, and he could find nothing to aim at.

"My only sorrow is that all my children wouldn't stay here and help," Ty Ty said slowly. "Buck and Shaw are still here helping me, and Buck's wife, and Darling Jill, but the other girl went off up to Augusta and got a job in a cotton mill across the river in Horse Creek Valley and married, and I reckon you know about Jim Leslie just as well as I could tell you. He's a big man up there in the city now, and he's as rich as the next one to come along."

12

"Yes, yes," Pluto said.

"Something got into Jim Leslie at an early age. He wouldn't have much to do with the rest of us, and still won't. Right now, he takes on like he don't know who I am. Just before his mother died, I took her up to the city one day to see him. She said she wanted to see him just one more time before she died. So I took her up there and went to his big white house on The Hill, and when he saw who it was at the door, he locked it and wouldn't let us in. I reckon that sort of hastened his mother's death, his acting that way, because she took sick and died before the week was out. He acted like he was ashamed of us, or something. And he still does. But the other girl is different. She's just like the rest of us. She's always pleased to see us when we go over to Horse Creek Valley to pay a call. I've always said that Rosamond was a right fine girl. Jim Leslie, though—I can't say so much for him. He's always looking the other way when I happen to meet him on the street in the city. He acts like he's ashamed of me. I can't see how that ought to be, though, because I'm his father."

"Yes, yes," Pluto said.

"I don't know why my oldest boy should turn out like that. I've always been a religious man, all my life I have. I've always done the best I could, no matter how much I was provoked, and I've tried to get my boys and girls to do the same. You see that piece of ground over yonder, Pluto? Well, that's God's little acre. I set aside an acre of my farm for God twenty-seven years ago, when I bought this place, and every year I give the church all that comes off that acre of ground. If it's cotton, I give the church all the money the cotton brings at market. The same with hogs, when I raised them, and about corn, too, when I plant it. That's God's little acre, Pluto. I'm proud to divide what little I have with God."

"What's growing on it this year?"

"Growing on it? Nothing, Pluto. Nothing but maybe beggar-lice and cockleburs now. I just couldn't find the time to plant cotton on it this year. Me and the boys and the darkies have been so busy with other things I just had to let God's little acre lie fallow for the time being."

Pluto sat up and looked across the field towards the pine woods. There were such great piles of excavated sand and clay heaped over the ground that it was difficult to see much further than a hundred yards without climbing a tree.

"Where'd you say that acre of land was, Ty Ty?"

"Over there near the woods. You won't be able to see much of it from here."

"Why did you put it 'way over there? Ain't that a sort of out-of-the-way place for it to be, Ty Ty?"

"Well, I'll tell you, Pluto. It ain't always been where it is now. I've been compelled to shift it around a heap during the past twenty-seven years. When the boys get to discussing where we'll start digging anew, it seems like it always falls on God's little acre. I don't know why that is, either. I'm set against digging on His ground, so I've been compelled to shift it around over the farm to keep from digging it up."

"You ain't scared of digging on it and striking a lode are you, Ty Ty?"

"No, I wouldn't say that, but I'd hate to have to see the lode struck on God's little acre the first thing, and be compelled to turn it all over to the church. That preacher's getting all he needs like it is. I'd hate something awful to have to give all the gold to him. I couldn't stand for that, Pluto."

Ty Ty raised his head and glanced across the field potted with holes. At one place he could see nearly a quarter of a mile away, in a straight line between the mounds of earth. Over there in the newground Black Sam and Uncle Felix were plowing the cotton. Ty Ty always managed to keep an eye on them, because he realized that if they did not raise any cotton and corn, there would be no money and little to eat that fall and winter. The Negroes had to be watched all the time, otherwise they would slip off at the first chance and dig in the holes behind their cabins.

"I've got something I'd like to ask you, Ty Ty."

"Is that what brought you out here in the hot sun?"

"I reckon so. I wanted to ask you."

"What's on your mind, Pluto? Go ahead and ask it."

"Your girl," Pluto said weakly, swallowing a little tobacco juice accidentally.

"Darling Jill?"

"Sure, that's why I came."

"What about her, Pluto?"

Pluto took the chew of tobacco out of his mouth and threw it aside. He coughed a little, trying to get the taste of the yellow tobacco out of his throat.

"I'd like to marry her."

"You would, Pluto? You mean it?"

"I sure to God would, Ty Ty. I'd go and cut off my right hand to marry her."

"You've taken a liking to her, Pluto?"

"I sure to God have," he said. "And that's a fact."

Ty Ty thought a while, pleased to think that his youngest daughter had attracted a man with serious intentions so early in life.

"No sense in cutting off your hand, Pluto. Just go ahead and marry her when she's ready for you. I reckon maybe you would consent to let her stay here some and help us dig after you are married, and maybe come yourself and help some. The more we have helping to dig, the quicker we're going to strike that lode, Pluto. I know you wouldn't object to digging some, being as how you would be one of the family."

"I never was one to dig much," Pluto said. "And that's a fact."

"Well, we won't discuss it any more just now. There'll be plenty of time to talk about it when you get married."

Pluto felt the blood running over his face just beneath his skin. He took out his handkerchief and wiped his face with it for a long time.

"But there's one thing about it——"

"What's that, Pluto?"

"Darling Jill said she didn't like me with such a fat belly. I can't help it, Ty Ty."

"What in the pluperfect hell has your belly got to do with it?" Ty Ty said. "Darling Jill is crazy some, Pluto. Don't pay no attention to what she says. Just go ahead and marry her and don't pay it no mind. She'll be all right after you get her off somewhere for a while. Darling Jill is crazy sometimes, and about nothing."

"And there was something else," Pluto said, turning his face away from Ty Ty.

"What is that?"

"I don't like to bring it up."

"Just go ahead and say it, Pluto, and after you've said it, it'll be done and can't be coming back to bother you."

"I heard that she ain't so particular about what she does sometimes."

"Just like what, for example?"

"Well, I heard that she's been teasing and fooling with a lot of men."

"Has things been said about my daughter, Pluto?"

"Well, about Darling Jill."

"What do people say, Pluto?"

"Nothing much, except that she's been teasing and fooling with a lot of men."

"I'm tickled to death to hear that. Darling Jill is the baby of the family, and she's coming along at last. I sure am glad to hear that."

"She ought to quit it, because I want to marry her."

"Never mind, Pluto," Ty Ty said. "Don't pay no heed to it. Don't give it no attention. She is careless, to be sure, but she don't mean no harm. She's just made that way. It don't hurt her none, not so that you will notice it, anyway. I reckon a lot of women are like that, a little or more, according to their natures. Darling Jill likes to tease a man some, but she don't mean no real harm. A pretty girl like Darling Jill has got everything coming her way, anyhow, and she knows it. It's up to you to satisfy her, Pluto, and make her so pleased she'll leave off with everybody but you. She's just been acting that way because she's come along now and there's been nobody man enough to hold her down. You're man enough to keep her satisfied. I can see that in your eyes, Pluto. Don't let that bother you no more."

"It's a pity God can't make a woman like Darling Jill and then leave off before He goes too far. That's what He did to her. He didn't know when He had made enough of a good thing. He just kept on and on—and now look at her! She's so full of teasing and the rest that I don't know that I'd ever have a peaceful night's rest when we get married."

"Well, it might be God's fault that He didn't know when to stop, Pluto, but just the same Darling Jill ain't the only girl He has made like that. In my time I've run across a heap like her. And I wouldn't have to go a thousand miles from home to cite you one. Now, you take Buck's wife, there. Pluto, I declare I don't know what to make of so pretty a girl as Griselda."

"That's what you think now, but I don't see how it can be so, Ty Ty. I've seen lots of women a little like her, but I've yet to see one that's as crazy as she is. When I get to be sheriff, I wouldn't want to have her running loose all the time like she does now. It wouldn't be good for my political career. I've got to keep that in mind."

"You ain't elected yet, Pluto."

"No, not yet, but everything is pointing my way. I've got a lot of friends working for me night and day all over the county. If somebody don't come along and shuffle the deck again, I'll get the office with no trouble at all."

"Tell them not to come here to my place, Pluto. I pledge you my vote, and all the votes on the place. Just be sure and don't let none of your workers come here trying to shake hands with everybody on the farm. I declare, there's been a hundred candidates here this summer, if there's been one. I won't shake with none of them, and I've told my boys and Darling Jill and Griselda not to stand for it. Ain't much use in telling you why I don't want candidates coming here, Pluto. Some of them are spreading the itch every which way, and it's going to stick for seven long years. I ain't saying you got the itch, but a heap of candidates do have. There's going to be so many cases of it in the county this fall and winter it won't be safe to go to town till the seven years have passed."

"There wouldn't be so many candidates for the few offices open, if it wasn't for the hard times. Hard times bring out the candidates just like lye does the fleas on a hound's back."

Over in the yard beside the house, Buck and Shaw had rolled the car out of the garage and were busy pumping up the tires. Buck's wife, Griselda, was standing in the shade of the porch talking to them. Darling Jill was not within sight.

"I've got to be getting along now," Pluto said. "I'm way behind this afternoon. I've got to make calls on all the voters between here and the crossroads between now and sundown. I've got to be going."

Pluto sat against the trunk of the live-oak tree, waiting until he felt like getting up. It was comfortable there, and shady; out in the field, where there was no shade, the sun beat down as steadily as ever. Even the weeds were beginning to curl a little in the steady heat.

"Where are we going to locate that albino you mentioned a while ago, Pluto?"

"You folks drive down below Clark's Mill and take the right-hand road at the creek. About a mile beyond that fork is where the fellow saw him. He was out in a thicket, on the edge of the swamp, cutting wood, the fellow said. Just get out and start looking. He's somewhere around there, because he couldn't get far away in this short time. If I didn't have so much to do, I'd go with you folks and help the little I could. The sheriff's race is getting hotter every day now, though, and I've got to count votes all the time I can. I don't know what I'd do if I didn't get elected."

"I reckon we'll find him all right," Ty Ty said. "I'll take the boys along, and they can do most of the walking while I sit and watch for signs. It'll be a pretty smart deal to take along some plow-lines to rope him with when we locate him. I reckon he'll try to put up a stiff scrap when I tell him to come along up here. But we'll get him through, if he's in the

country. We've been needing just what he is for the longest
time. The darkies said an all-white man can divine a lode, and
I reckon they know what they're talking about. They dig more
of the time than me and the boys, and we're at it from daybreak to sundown most days. If Shaw hadn't got that notion to
quit and go to town just a while ago, we'd be at it now, down
in that big hole yonder."

Pluto made as if to rise, but the effort discouraged him. He
sat back again breathing hard, to rest a little longer.

"I wouldn't be too rough with that albino, Ty Ty," he
advised. "I don't know what you're aiming to catch him with,
so I can't say how to go about it, but I sure don't advise shoot-
ing him with a gun. Hurting him would be against the law, and
if I was you folks I'd play safe and not hurt him no more than
I could help. You need him here to help you too bad to take
any chances on running up against the law needlessly, just
when you've gone and caught what you need most right now.
Just catch him as easy as you can, so he won't get hurt and
have scars to show for the handling."

"He won't get hurt none," Ty Ty promised. "I'll be as
gentle with him as I would a newborn babe. I need that albino
too bad to be rough with him."

"I've got to be getting along now," Pluto said, still not
moving.

"Ain't it hot, though?" Ty Ty said, looking out at the heat
on the baked earth.

It made Pluto hot to think about it. He closed his eyes, but
that made him feel no cooler.

"It's too hot to be out counting votes today," Pluto said.
"And that's a fact."

They sat a while longer, watching Buck and Shaw working
over the big automobile in the yard beside the house. Griselda
sat on the porch steps and watched them. Darling Jill was still
not within sight.

"We'll be needing all the help we can find after we rope
that albino and get him home," Ty Ty said. "I reckon I'll have
to put Darling Jill and Griselda to digging, too. I wish Rosamond was here. She could help us out a lot. Do you reckon
you could come by here in a day or two and dig a little with
us, Pluto? It would be a big help, if you would dig some. I can't
say how much I would be obliged to you, for whatever digging
you want to do."

"I've got to be out and electioneering, Ty Ty," Pluto said,
shaking his head. "Those other candidates for sheriff are tear-

ing up the patch night and day. I've got to keep after the voters every minute I can spare. These voters are queer people, Ty Ty. One will promise to vote for you, and then the first thing you know, he's promising the next fellow to come along the very same thing. I can't afford to lose this election. I declare, I wouldn't have a thing to do for a living, if I lost it. I can't afford to lose a good job like that when I haven't a thing to do for a living."

"How many men running against you, Pluto?"

"For sheriff?"

"That's what I meant to say."

"There was eleven in the race when I last heard about it this morning, and by night there's liable to be two or three more. But the actual candidates are few besides all the workers they've got counting votes for them, expecting to be made deputies. Looks like now every time you go up to a voter and ask a man to vote for you it sort of puts a bug in his ear and the first thing you know, he's out running for some office himself. If these hard times don't slacken before fall, there's going to be so many candidates running for county offices that there won't be a common ordinary voter left."

Pluto was beginning to wish he had not left the shaded streets in town to come out into the country and bake in the hot sun. He had hoped that he would see Darling Jill, but now that he could not find her, he was thinking of returning to town without calling on the voters along the road.

"If you can get a little time off, Pluto, I wish you would come out this way in a day or two and give us a hand with a shovel. It'll help us a lot. And while you're digging, you ought not to forget about the three or four votes here on the place. Votes are things you are in need of right now."

"I'll try to come by some time soon, and if I do I'll try to dig a little for you, if the hole ain't too deep. I don't want to get down in something I can't get out of again. After you get that albino you won't have to work so hard, anyway. When you catch him, all your troubles are over, Ty Ty, and all you'll have to do will be to dig down and strike the lode."

"I wish it was so," Ty Ty said. "I've been digging fifteen years now, and I need a little encouragement."

"An albino can locate it," Pluto said. "And that's a fact."

"The boys are ready to start," Ty Ty said, getting up. "We've got to be up and on our way before night sets in. I aim to rope that all-white man before daybreak."

Ty Ty started down the path towards the house where his

sons were waiting. He did not look back to see if Pluto had got up, because he was in a big hurry. Pluto got up slowly and followed Ty Ty down the path between the deep holes and the high mounds of earth toward his car where he had left it in the road in front of the house two hours before. He hoped he would see Darling Jill before he left, but she was not within sight.

Chapter III

WHEN TY TY AND PLUTO reached the house, they found the boys resting after their work. All the tires were tight and hard, and the radiator was filled to overflowing. Everything seemed to be ready for the trip. While waiting for their father to get ready to start, Shaw sat on the runningboard rolling a cigarette, and Buck sat on the steps beside his wife with his arm around her waist. Griselda was playing with his hair, ruffling it with her hands.

"Here he comes now," Griselda said, "but that's no sign he's ready to leave."

"Boys," Ty Ty said, walking over to the sycamore stump and sitting down to rest, "we've got to be up and doing. I aim to rope that all-white man before daybreak tomorrow morning. If he's in the country, we'll have him roped by then, if we don't catch him a heap sooner."

"You'll have to keep guard over him when you bring him back, won't you, Pa?" Griselda asked. "The darkies might try to take him off, as soon as they hear that you've got a conjurman on the place."

"Now you be quiet, Griselda," Ty Ty said angrily. "You know good and well I don't take any stock in superstition and conjur and such things. We're going about this thing scientifically, and no fooling around with conjur. It takes a man of science to strike a lode. You've never heard of darkies digging up many nuggets with all their smart talk about conjur. It just can't be done. I'm running this business scientifically clear from the start. Now you be quiet, Griselda."

"The darkies get nuggets somewhere," Buck said. "I've seen plenty of them, and they come out of the ground some way. The darkies would catch an albino if they knew there was one in the county, or anywhere near. They would try to catch him, if they weren't too scared to go after him."

Ty Ty turned away, tired of arguing with them. He knew what he was going to do, but he was too exhausted after a hard day's work out in the big hole to try to convince them of his way of looking at it. He turned around and looked in another direction.

It was late in the afternoon, but the sun looked as if it were a mile high, and it was every bit as hot as it had ever been.

"Sorry I've got to rush right off like this, folks," Pluto said, sitting down on the shaded steps. "There's a ballot box full of votes between here and the crossroads, and I've got to count them all before sundown tonight. It never does pay to put things off. That's why I've got to rush off like this in the heat of the day."

Shaw and Buck looked at Pluto a moment and at Griselda, and laughed out loud. Pluto would not have noticed them if they had not kept on laughing.

"What's so funny, Buck?" he asked, looking around him in the yard, and finally down at his overflowing belly.

Griselda began laughing again when she saw him looking down at himself.

Buck nudged her with his elbow, urging her to answer Pluto.

"Mr. Swint," she said, "it looks like you will have to wait till tomorrow to count some more votes. Darling Jill went off down the road about an hour ago and she hasn't come back yet. She was driving your car."

Pluto shook himself like a dog that has been standing in the rain. He made as though to get up, but he could not rise from the steps. He looked across the yard where he had left his car earlier in the afternoon, and it was not there. He could not see it anywhere.

Ty Ty leaned forward to hear what they were talking about.

Pluto had had plenty of time to make some reply, but he had uttered no intelligible sound. He was in a position where he did not know what to say or to do. He merely sat where he was and said nothing.

"Mr. Swint," Griselda said, "Darling Jill went off in your automobile."

"It's gone," he said weakly. "And that's a fact."

"Don't pay no attention to Darling Jill," Ty Ty said consolingly. "Pluto, Darling Jill is as crazy as hell sometimes, and about nothing."

Pluto sank back on the steps, his body spreading on the boards when he relaxed. He took a fresh chew of yellow plug. There was nothing else he could do.

"We ought to be starting, Pa," Shaw said. "It's getting late."

"Why, son," he said, "I thought you quit work an hour or two ago to go to town. What about that game of pool you were going to shoot?"

"I wasn't going to town to shoot pool. I'd rather go to the swamp tonight."

"Well, then, if you didn't aim to shoot pool in town tonight, what about that woman you would be after?"

Shaw walked away without a reply. When Ty Ty tried to make fun of him, he could only walk away. He could not explain things to his father, and he had long before decided that the best course was to let him go ahead and talk as much as he wished.

"It's time to get started," Buck said.

"That ain't no lie," Ty Ty said, going down toward the barn.

He came back in a few moments carrying several plowlines over his arm. He tossed the ropes into the back seat of the car and sat down on the stump again.

"Boy," he said, "I've just had a notion. I'm going to send for Rosamond and Will to come over here. We need them to help us dig some, now that we're going to have that albino to show us where the lode is, and Rosamond and Will ain't doing much now. The mill over there at Scottsville is shut down again, and Will ain't doing a thing in the world. He might just as well be over here helping us dig. Rosamond and Griselda can help a lot, and maybe Darling Jill, too. Now mind you, I don't say I'm asking girls to do work like the rest of us. They can do a lot to help us, though. They can cook food for us and carry water, and some other things. Griselda there, and Rosamond will help all they can, but I ain't so sure about Darling Jill. I'll try to persuade her to do something for us out there in the holes. I wouldn't let a girl on my place work like a man, but I'll do my durndest trying to make Darling Jill want to help some."

"I'd just like to see you make Will Thompson dig," Shaw said, jerking his head at his father. "That Will Thompson is the laziest white man this side of Atlanta. I've never seen him work, not here, anyway. I don't know what he does over there in that cotton mill, when it's running, but I'll bet it's nothing to speak of. Will Thompson won't be doing much digging, even if he does go down in a hole and go through the motion of it."

"You boys don't seem to catch on to Will like I do. Now, Will is just as hard a worker as the next one. The reason he never likes to dig in the holes here for us is because he don't feel at home here. Will is a cotton mill man, and he can't get along in the country on a farm. But maybe Will will dig some this time. Will can dig as good as the next one, if he wants to. He might get the gold-fever over here this time, and go down in the ground and dig like nobody's business. You never can tell what will happen when the fever strikes a man; maybe you'll wake up some morning and go out there to find him digging for a fare-you-well. I ain't seen a man or a woman yet who won't get down in the ground and dig when the gold-fever strikes him. You get to thinking about turning up a handful of those little yellow nuggets, maybe with the next stroke of the pick; and—man alive—you dig and dig and dig! That's why I'm going to send for Rosamond and Will right away. We'll be needing all the help we can get, son. That lode might be thirty feet in the ground, and at a place we haven't started digging into yet."

"It might be on God's little acre," Buck said. "What would you do about that? You wouldn't dig nuggets when they were all going to the preacher and the church, would you? I know I wouldn't. All the gold I get is going into my pockets, at least my share of it. I wouldn't be giving it to the preacher at the church."

"We ought to give up that piece of ground till we can dig on it and make sure," Shaw said. "God's not in need of it, and the first thing you know, we're going to strike a lode on it. I'll be dog-goned if I'm going to dig for nuggets and see that preacher get them. I'm in favor of shifting that piece of land till we can see what's in it."

"All right, boys," Ty Ty agreed, "I'll move it again, but I ain't aiming to do away with God's little acre altogether. It's His and I can't take it away from Him after twenty-seven years. That wouldn't be right. But there ain't nothing wrong with shifting it a little, if need be. It would be a heathen shame to strike the lode on it, to be sure, the first thing, and I reckon I'd better shift it so we won't be bothered."

"Why don't you put it over here where the house and barn are, Pa?" Griselda suggested. "There's nothing under this house, and you can't be digging under it, anyway."

"I never thought of doing that, Griselda," Ty Ty said, "but it sure sounds fine to me. I reckon I'll shift it over here. Now, I'm pretty much glad to get that off my mind."

Pluto turned his head and looked at Ty Ty.

"You haven't shifted it already, have you, Ty Ty?" he asked.

"Shifted it already? Why, sure. This is God's little acre we're sitting on right now. I moved it from over yonder to right here."

"You're the quickest man of action I've ever heard about," Pluto said, shaking his head. "And that's a fact."

Buck and Griselda went around the corner of the house out of sight. Shaw started to follow them, but he changed his mind and rolled a cigarette instead. He was ready to go on the trip, and he did not wish to delay the start any longer. He knew, though, that Ty Ty would not leave until he became tired of sitting still.

Pluto sat on the steps thinking of Darling Jill and wondering where she was. He wished she would return so he could sit beside her and put his arms around her. Sometimes she would let him sit beside her, and at other times she would not. She was as inconsistent about that as she was about everything else she did. Pluto did not know what to do about it; she was that kind of girl, and he knew of no way to change her. But as long as she would sit still and let him hug her, he was completely satisfied; it was when she slapped him on the face and hit him in the belly with her fists that he was wholly displeased.

An automobile passed the house in a cloud of red dust, powdering the roadside until the weeds and trees looked more dead than ever. Pluto glanced at the car, but he quickly saw that Darling Jill was not driving it, and he had no further interest in it. The car went out of sight around the bend in the road, but the dust lingered in the air long after it had gone.

The last time he had seen Darling Jill she had made him leave five minutes after he got there. It hurt Pluto, and he went back home and got into bed. He had come to see her for the evening that time, confidently expecting to be with her for several hours at least, but five minutes after he reached the house he was on his way home again. Darling Jill had told him to go roll his hoop. On top of that she slapped him on the face and hit him in the belly with her fists. Now he hoped that if there was a law of averages, or even a law of compensation, his meeting of her this time would be wholly different. This time she should, if there was any justice, be glad to see him; she should even let him hug her and, to make up for the previous visit, allow him to kiss her several times. Darling Jill should do all of that, but whether she would or not was something he did not know. Darling Jill was as uncertain as were his chances of being elected sheriff that fall.

The thought of the coming election stirred Pluto. He made

as though to stand up, but he did not move from his seat. He could not get out in the heat of the day and walk down the dusty road calling on voters.

Buck and Griselda came back with two large Senator Watson watermelons and a salt-shaker. Buck also had a butcher-knife in his hand. Pluto forgot his troubles when he saw the two large melons, and sat up. Ty Ty pulled himself out of his crouched position. After Buck and Griselda had put the melons on the porch. Ty Ty went over and cut them into quarters.

Griselda carried Pluto his portion, and he thanked her many times over for her consideration. There would have been no need for his getting up to go for his slice of watermelon inasmuch as Griselda was already standing. And if she had not brought it to him, he did not know whether he could have gone after it or not. She had sat down beside him and was watching him lower his face into the cool meat. The melons had been cooling on the bottom of the well for two days and they were ice-cold.

"Mr. Swint," she said, looking up at Pluto, "your eyes look like watermelon seeds."

Everyone laughed. Pluto knew she was right. He could almost see himself at that moment.

"Now, Griselda," he said, "you're just making fun of me again."

"I couldn't help saying it, Mr. Swint. Your eyes are so small and your face is so red, that you do look exactly like a watermelon with two seeds showing."

Ty Ty laughed again, louder than before.

"There's a time for fun, and a time for work," he said, spitting out a mouthful of seeds, "and now is the time for work. We've got to be up and doing, boys. We've sat around the house here long enough for one day, and now we've got to be on our way. I aim to rope that albino sometime between now and daybreak tomorrow morning. Let's be up and doing."

Pluto wiped his hands and face and laid the rind aside. He wished to wink at Griselda, and to lay his hand on her knees. In a minute or two he found the courage to wink at her with his watermelon seeds, but try as he might he could not bring himself to touch her. The thought of laying his hand on her knees and maybe trying to push his fingers between her legs brought a blush to his face and neck. He drummed on the steps with his fingers in seven-eighths time, whistling under his breath, and scared to death that somebody would read his thoughts.

"Buck's got a fine-looking wife, hasn't he, Pluto?" Ty Ty asked him, spitting out another mouthful of watermelon seeds. "Did you ever see a finer-looking girl anywhere in the country? Just look at that creamy skin and that gold in her hair, not to mention all that pale blueness in her eyes. And while I'm praising her, I can't overlook the rest of her. I reckon Griselda is the prettiest of them all. Griselda has the finest pair of rising beauties a man can ever hope to see. It's a wonder that God ever put such prettiness in the house with an onery old cuss like me. Maybe I don't deserve to see it, but I'm here to tell you I'm going to take my fill of looking while I can."

Griselda hung her head and blushed.

"Aw, now, Pa," she begged.

"Ain't I right, Pluto?"

"She's a perfect little female," Pluto said. "And that's a fact."

Griselda glanced up at Buck and blushed again. Buck laughed at her.

"Son," Ty Ty said, turning to Buck, "wherever in the world did you happen to find her, you lucky dog?"

"Well, there's no more where she came from," he said. "She was the pick of the crop."

"And I'll bet they've given up trying to raise any more, there at that place, after seeing you come and take away the beauty of them all."

"Now stop that, Pa, you and Buck," Griselda said, putting her hands over her face and trying to keep them from seeing her.

"I hate to cross you, Griselda," Ty Ty said determinedly. "Once I get started about you, I can't stop. I've just got to praise you. And I reckon any man would who has seen you like I have. The first time I saw you, when Buck brought you here from wherever it was you came from, I felt like getting right down there and then and licking something. That's a rare feeling to come over a man, and when I have it, it does me proud to talk about it for you to hear."

"Please, Pa," she said.

Ty Ty continued talking, but it was impossible for anyone to hear what he was saying. He sat on the stump talking to himself and looking down at the hard white sand at his feet.

Pluto moved his hands a little. He wished to get closer to Griselda, but he was afraid. He turned around to see if anyone was looking. The others were all looking elsewhere, and he quickly put his hand on her legs and leaned against her.

Griselda turned and slapped him so quickly he did not know what had struck him. He felt the flow of blood rushing to his stinging cheeks and he heard the tingle of bells in his ears. When he could open his eyes and look up, Griselda was standing on the ground in front of him, and Buck and Shaw were doubled up with laughter.

"I'll teach you not to get fresh with me, you big haystack!" she cried angrily. "Don't get me confused with Darling Jill. She may not always slap you, but I certainly shall. You'll know better than to try something like that again."

Ty Ty got up and came across the yard, looking at Pluto to see how badly he was hurt.

"Pluto didn't mean no harm, Griselda," Ty Ty said, trying to calm her. "Pluto wouldn't harm you, not with Buck around, anyhow."

"You'd better be going on down the road to count your votes, Mr. Swint," she said.

"Now, Griselda, you know good and well Pluto can't leave till Darling Jill comes back with his car."

"He can walk, can't he?" she asked, laughing at Pluto. "I didn't know he had got so he can't even walk any more."

Pluto looked around him frantically, as if he were looking for something to hold on to. The thought of getting out into the hot sun and walking in the red dust terrified him. He clutched the overlapping boards of the steps with both hands.

Shaw noticed someone coming towards the house from the barn. He looked again a moment later and saw that it was Black Sam. When the colored man came closer, Shaw left the yard and went to meet him.

"Mr. Shaw," Black Sam said, taking off his hat, "I'd like pretty much to have a word with your Pa. I need to see him."

"What do you want to see him about? I told you what he said about the rations."

"I know you did, Mr. Shaw, but I'm still hungry. I'd like to see your Pa, please, sir, boss."

Shaw called Ty Ty to the corner of the house.

"Mr. Ty Ty, I'm all out of something to eat at my house, and we ain't had nothing to eat all today. My old woman is downright hungry for something to eat."

"What in the pluperfect hell do you mean by coming to the house and bothering me, Black Sam?" Ty Ty shouted. "I sent you word that I'd get you some food when I get around to it. You can't come here to the house and bother me like this. Now get on home and stop worrying me. I'm going off to rope an all-white man tonight, and I've got to give all my thoughts to that. This all-white man is going to help me locate the lode."

"You ain't speaking of a conjur-man, is you, Mr. Ty Ty?" Black Sam asked fearfully. "Mr. Ty Ty, please, sir, white-folks, don't bring no conjur-man here, Mr. Ty Ty, please, sir, boss, I can't stand to see a conjur-man."

"Shut up, durn it," Ty Ty said. "It's none of your business what I do. Now go on home and stop coming here to the house when I'm busy."

The colored man backed away. He forgot for the time being about his hunger. The thought of seeing an albino on the place made him breathless.

"Now, wait a minute," Ty Ty said. "If you butcher that mule and eat him while I'm gone, when I get back I'll make you pay for him, and it won't be in money either, because I know you ain't got a penny."

"No, sir, Mr. Ty Ty, I wouldn't do nothing like that. I wouldn't eat up your mule, boss. I never thought of anything like that. But, please, sir, white captain, don't bring no con-jur-man around here."

Black Sam backed away from Ty Ty. His eyes were ab-normally large and extraordinarily white.

When Ty Ty had turned and gone back to the front yard, Shaw went up to the colored man.

"After we leave," he said, "come around to the back door and Miss Griselda will give you something out of the kitchen. Tell Uncle Felix to come and get something, too."

Black Sam thanked him, but he did not remember hearing a word Shaw had said. He turned and ran towards the barn, moaning to himself.

Chapter IV

BUCK WALKED BACK and forth between the porch and the car impatiently.

"Let's get started, Pa," he said. "We'll be tramping around in the swamp all night if we don't get an early start. I don't like the swamps much after dark, anyway."

"I thought you were going to send for Rosamond and Will," Griselda broke in, looking at her father-in-law. "You'd better write the letter now and mail it when you go through town."

"I didn't aim to mail a letter," Ty Ty said. "A letter would take too long to get there. I figured on sending after them. I reckon Darling Jill could go over there to Scottsville and bring them back all right. I'll send her on the bus to Augusta, and she'll get there early tonight. They could all start back tomorrow morning on the bus and maybe get here in time to start digging in the afternoon just as soon as dinner was over."

"Darling Jill isn't here," Buck said. "There's no way of knowing when she'll be back, either. If we have to wait for her, we'll never get started to the swamp."

Pluto sat up erectly and looked down the road. He would never get around to make a personal call on the voters at the rate he was going.

"She'll be back any minute now," Ty Ty said assuredly. "We'll wait and take her to Marion with us. When we get to town, we'll leave her at the bus station and go on to the swamp after that albino. That's the thing to do. Darling Jill will be home any minute now. Wouldn't be any sense in going off and leaving when she'll be here before long."

Buck shrugged his shoulders and walked up and down in the yard disgustedly. Two hours had already been wasted, and nothing had been accomplished by the delay.

"I would—" Pluto said, and then he hesitated.

"You'd do what?" Ty Ty asked him.

"Well, I was going to say——"

"Say what? Go on, Pluto. Speak your mind. We're all of a family here."

"If she wouldn't object, I thought——"

"What in the pluperfect hell has got into you, Pluto?" Ty Ty asked angrily. "You start out to say something, and then you get all red in the face and neck, and you carry on like you're scared to say it and scared not to. Go on and tell me what it is."

Pluto's face got red again. He looked from person to person, at last taking out his handkerchief and holding it over his face while he pretended to wipe it. When his face became less inflamed, he put it back into his pocket.

"I was going to say that I'd be pleased to drive Darling Jill over to Horse Creek Valley this evening, if she would bring my car back. I mean, I'd be pleased to take her over there if she'd let me."

"Why, that's real neighborly of you, Pluto," Ty Ty said enthusiastically. "Now I know you can count on our votes. If you'll take her over there, it'll save me some money in the end.

I'll tell her to go with you. She won't mind it at all. What do you mean by saying if she'll let you? I'll tell her to, Pluto. Much obliged for the offer. I'll save a lot of money in the end by that deal."

"Do you reckon she'll go with me—I mean, do you reckon she'll consent to letting me drive her over there in my car if she brings it back?"

"I reckon she will when I tell her to go, and she ought to be real pleased to have you taking her," Ty Ty said emphatically, spitting upon a wild onion stem at his feet. "Don't make the mistake of thinking I ain't got a hand over my own children, Pluto. She'll go, all right, when I tell her to go. She won't mind it a bit."

"If Pluto is going to take her, then let's get started for the swamps, Pa," Buck said. "It's getting late. I want to get back here by midnight, if I can."

"Boys," Ty Ty said, "I'm mighty proud to hear you say you want to be up and doing. We'll start right off. Pluto, you drive Darling Jill over to Scottsville and leave her with Rosamond and Will. It's mighty fine of you. I'm mighty much obliged to you, Pluto."

Ty Ty ran up the porch steps and back to the yard again. He had forgotten for a moment how excited he was over the prospect of finding the albino.

"Griselda, when Darling Jill gets back, tell her to go over to Horse Creek Valley and bring Rosamond and Will back tomorrow morning. She'll have to explain what we want with them, and you can tell her what to say to them. We need them to help us dig. Tell Darling Jill that me and the boys have gone to the swamp after that all-white man, and tell her we're going to strike the lode in no time. I won't say when, but I can say in no time. I'll buy you and her both the finest clothes the merchants in the city can show. I'll get the same for Rosamond, when we strike the lode. I want Rosamond and Will to know we need their help pretty bad, so they'll come tomorrow and help us. We'll all start in as soon as dinner is over tomorrow, and dig and dig and dig."

Ty Ty fumbled in his pocket a moment, at length taking out a quarter and handing it to Griselda.

"Take this and buy yourself a pretty the next time you go to town," he urged. "I wish I had more to give you, because you're so much prettiness and when I look at you, I can't help it, but we ain't struck the lode yet."

"Let's get going, Pa," Shaw said.

Buck cranked up the big seven-passenger car and idled the engine while his father was giving Griselda final instructions for Darling Jill. Just when Buck thought Ty Ty was ready to get into the car, he wheeled around and ran down to the barn. A few moments later he came running back with three or four more plow-lines. He tossed them into the back seat with the others.

Ty Ty stood looking at Pluto on the steps for several minutes, his brow wrinkled, intent upon him as if he were trying to remember something he had meant to tell him before leaving. Unable to recall it, he turned and climbed into the car with Buck and Shaw. Buck raced the engine, and a cloud of black smoke blew out of the exhaust pipe. Ty Ty turned around in his seat and waved good-by to Griselda and Pluto.

"Be sure and remember to tell Darling Jill what I told you," he said. "And tell her to come home the first thing tomorrow morning without fail."

Shaw had to reach over his father and shut the door that Ty Ty had been too excited to close. With a roar and a rank odor from the exhaust pipe, the big car shot out of the yard and rumbled into the highway. They were out of sight a moment later.

"I hope they find that albino," Pluto said, not particularly to Griselda. "If they don't find him, Ty Ty will come back swearing I lied about him. I swear to God, the fellow said he saw him down there. I didn't lie about it. The fellow said he saw him in the thicket on the edge of the swamp cutting wood as big as life. If Ty Ty doesn't find him and bring him home, he'll take his vote away from me. That'll be real bad. And that's a fact."

Griselda had gone to the porch while Pluto was talking. She could not hear what he was mumbling to himself, for one thing; and she did not care to stand out in the yard with him, for another. She sat down in a rocker and watched the back of Pluto's head. From the position she was in, she could get a better view of the road, and she watched for the first sign of Darling Jill's returning home.

Pluto sat alone on the steps mumbling something to himself. He no longer raised his voice high enough for her to hear what he was saying. He was thinking of what Ty Ty Walden would say and do if he could not find the albino. He was beginning to feel sorry that he had ever mentioned the albino in the first place. He knew then that he should have kept his mouth shut about something he was not certain of.

Griselda stood up and looked down the road.

"Is that your car, Pluto?" she asked, pointing over his head towards the cloud of red dust rising from the road. "It looks like Darling Jill driving it, anyway."

Pluto got to his feet with effort. He stood up and took several steps in that direction. He waited beside the sycamore stump while the automobile came closer. It was making a lot of noise, but it did look like his car. He wondered why it was making so much noise. He had never noticed it when he drove.

"Yes," Griselda said. "That's Darling Jill, Pluto. Can't you recognize your own automobile?"

Darling Jill turned into the yard without slackening speed. The heavy sedan skidded a distance of ten or twelve feet, coming to an abrupt stop turned half-way around in the yard. One of the rear tires was as flat as a board, and the innertube, which was hanging from the rim, had been chewed all to pieces. Pluto looked at the tire with a feeling of great fatigue coming over him.

Pluto heard Griselda coming down the steps behind him and he moved out of her way a little.

"You had a puncture, Pluto," Darling Jill said. "See it?"

Pluto tried to say something, and he found that it was difficult to pull his tongue loose from the roof of his mouth. When it finally came loose, it fell between his lips and hung on the outside.

"What's the matter with you?" she asked, jumping out to the ground. "Can't you see it? You're not blind, are you?"

"Who had a puncture?" Pluto managed to ask. He realized how weak his voice was only after he had spoken. "Who?"

"You did, you big horse's ass," Darling Jill said. "What's the matter with you? Can't you see anything?"

Griselda came running up.

"Hush, Darling Jill," she said. "Don't talk like that."

As soon as Pluto could recover, he began jacking up the wheel to change the spare on to it. He went about replacing the punctured tire, puffing and blowing, but he did not have a word to say to Darling Jill for rim-cutting a brand new tire and chewing up a new two-dollar innertube. Darling Jill watched him at work a moment, laughed at him, and started to the porch with Griselda.

"Who's been eating melons, and didn't save me some?"

"There's plenty left," Griselda said. "I saved you two large pieces in the kitchen."

"What is Pluto Swint doing around here?"

"Pa wants you to go over to Rosamond and Will's and bring them back," Griselda said, quickly remembering Ty Ty's messages. "Pa and Buck and Shaw have gone to the swamp to catch an albino to divine the lode for them, and he said he needs Rosamond and Will to help dig. Pluto will take you over there right away, and Pa said you and Rosamond and Will can come back tomorrow morning on the first bus. I wish I could go, too."

"Come on and go. Why can't you?"

"Buck said he might be back by midnight, and I want to be here when he comes home. I'll go over there some other time. You'd better hurry and dress."

"I'll be ready in a minute," Darling Jill said. "I've got to take a bath first, though. Don't let Pluto go off and leave me. I'll be ready in no time. It won't take me long."

"Oh, he'll wait for you," Griselda said, following her into the house. "He'll be here, all right. You couldn't pry him loose until you're ready to go with him."

She and Darling Jill went into the house, leaving Pluto alone in the yard to change the tire. He had already got the punctured tire off the wheel, and he was getting ready to put the spare on and tighten the lugs. He worked away in the heat, not mindful of the fact that Griselda and Darling Jill had left him alone in the yard.

When he had finished and had replaced the jack and lug wrench under the seat, he stood up and tried to dust his clothes. His face and arms were covered with dirt and perspiration, and his hands were grimy. He tried for a while to wipe it off with his handkerchief, but he had to give that up when he saw how hopeless it was. He started around the house to the well in the back yard where he could bathe his face and hands.

Pluto reached the corner of the house without raising his eyes from the ground. When he got to the corner, he looked up and saw Darling Jill in the yard.

First, he stepped back for a moment; then, he stepped forward again and looked at her the second time. After that he did not know what to do.

Griselda was sitting on the top step at the porch talking to Darling Jill. She had not looked in Pluto's direction. Darling Jill was standing over a large white enameled tub that had been hurriedly carried to the yard from the house and placed halfway between the porch and the well. She was busy talking to Griselda and soaping her arms when Pluto saw her.

It was at that moment when Pluto realized fully where he was. He did not wish to turn around and leave, but he was afraid to go closer.

"Well, darn my socks!" Pluto said, his mouth agape.

Darling Jill heard him and she looked at him. She paused with the soapy washcloth on her shoulder, and looked even more intently than before. Griselda turned to see what she was staring at so long.

For a while, Pluto thought that perhaps Darling Jill was trying to stare him out of countenance, or perhaps drive him back around the house, but he had remained there several minutes already, and he did not know what she intended to do. He was determined, after having stood there that long, to make her take the first move. Darling Jill did not attempt to run from his sight, and she did not try to cover herself with the washcloth or with anything else. She just stood over the white enameled bowl, staring at him.

"Well, darn my socks!" Pluto said again. "And that's a fact."

Darling Jill reached down into the bowl with both hands and, picking up all the suds she could hold, threw the soapy froth at Pluto. Pluto, only a few feet away, saw the suds coming towards him, but he could not force his body to move in time to escape them. By the time he finally moved a few steps, the soap was already stinging his eyes and running down the collar of his shirt. He could not see a thing. Somewhere in front of him he could hear both Griselda and Darling Jill laughing, but he was unable to protest. When he opened his mouth to say something, he tasted soap all over his tongue, and the inside of his mouth tasted just as disagreeable. He bent as far forward as he could and tried to spit out the taste of the soap.

"That will darn your socks," he heard Darling Jill say to him. "Maybe you'll think twice the next time you try to slip up on me while I'm naked. What can you see now, Pluto? See anything, Pluto? Why don't you look at me now—you could see something if you did!"

Griselda laughed at him again on the steps.

"I wish I could take a picture of him now," she said to Darling Jill. "He would make a pretty picture to show the voters on election day, wouldn't he, Darling Jill? I'd call it the 'Soapy Sheriff of Wayne County Counting Votes.'"

"If he ever tries to slip up on me again while I'm naked, I'll duck him in a tub of suds until he learns to cry 'Uncle' in three languages. I never saw such a man in all my life. He's always trying to put his hands on me and squeeze something, or else trying to sneak up and grab me while I'm naked. I never saw such a man."

"Maybe he didn't know you were taking a bath in the back yard. Darling Jill. He wouldn't know it until he came around here and saw you."

"Don't you think he didn't know it. If you think that, then tell me why it is he comes around the corner of the house every time I'm taking one. Pluto isn't so dumb as he looks. He'll fool you by his looks."

There was a silence after that, and Pluto knew they had left the yard and gone into the house. He wrung his handkerchief again and attempted to wipe the soap out of his eyes. Feeling his way around to the front of the house, he reached the steps and sat down to wait for Darling Jill to dress and come out. He was not angry with her for throwing soap in his face; nothing could have made him angry with her. She had done things much worse than that to him many times. And she called him the worst names she could think of.

When he succeeded in drying the soap and in wiping the last of it from his face and hair, he was surprised to look up and see that the sun was almost down. He realized that he would not be able to call on any more of the voters that day. But as long as he was taking Darling Jill to Scottsville, he did not regret it. He would rather be with her than win an election.

The screendoor behind him squeaked, and Darling Jill and Griselda came out.

They stood on the porch at his back looking down at the top of his head and giggling a little. He could not turn around to see them without getting up, and he decided to wait until they came down the steps before looking at them.

"Darning your socks, aren't you, Pluto?" Darling Jill asked him. "You should have done that before you went around to the back yard."

Chapter V

IT WAS AFTER ten o'clock when they reached Scottsville that evening. Pluto was lost in the maze of mill streets, but Darling Jill had been there many times before and she recognized the house before they got to it. Rosamond and Will's house was apparently like all the others, but Rosamond usually had blue curtains over the windows and Darling Jill had looked for those.

Pluto stopped the car but did not shut off the motor. Darling Jill turned the switch and took out the key.

"Wait a minute," Pluto said excitedly. "Don't do that, Darling Jill."

She dropped the key into her pocketbook and laughed at Pluto's protests. Before he could stop her, she had opened the door and stepped to the street. Pluto got out and followed her up the walk to the front door.

"I don't hear Will anywhere," she said, stopping and trying to see through the window.

They opened the door and went into the hall. The light was burning and all the other doors were open. From one of the rooms came the sound of someone crying. Darling Jill went into one of the dark rooms and snapped on the light. Rosamond was lying across the bed with part of a sheet covering her face. She was sobbing loudly.

"Rosamond!" Darling Jill cried. "What in the world is the matter!"

She ran and fell across the bed with her sister.

Rosamond raised herself on her elbows and looked around the room. She dried the tears on her face and tried to smile.

"I wasn't expecting you," she said, throwing her arms around Darling Jill and bursting into tears again. "I'm glad you came when you did. I thought I was going to die. I must have been out of my head a little."

"What did Will do to you? Where is he?"

Pluto had been standing in the doorway, not knowing what else to do. He tried not to look at Rosamond until she had noticed him.

"Hello, Pluto," she smiled. "I certainly am glad to see you again. Take the clothes off the chair and sit down and make yourself at home."

"Where's Will?" Darling Jill asked again. "Tell me what happened, Rosamond."

"I suppose he's down the street somewhere," Rosamond said. "I don't know exactly where he is."

"But what's the matter?"

"He's been drunk all this week," Rosamond said. "And he won't stay at home with me. He talks about turning the power on at the mill when he's drunk, and when he's sober, he won't say anything. The last time he came home he hit me."

Her face was badly swollen. One of her eyes was slightly discolored, and blood had been flowing from her nose.

"Isn't he working?"

"No, of course not. The mill is still shut down. I don't know when it will start running again. Some people say it never will. I don't know."

Pluto stood up, twisting his hat in his hands.

"I've got to be getting back home," he said. "And that's a fact."

"Sit down, Pluto," Darling Jill told him. "And be quiet."

He sat down again, placing his hat under the chair and folding his hands in his lap.

"I came over to take you and Will home with me," Darling Jill said. "Pa says he wants you and Will to help some. He needs Will to help dig, and you can do whatever you like. Pa's got something on his mind about finding gold for sure this time. I don't know what got into him."

"Oh, he always has some new notion," Rosamond said. "There's no gold on that place, is there? If there was gold there, they would have found it long before now. Why can't he stop digging the land full of holes and farm some?"

"I don't know," Darling Jill said. "He and the boys think they're going to strike it soon. That's what keeps them at it all the time. I wish they would."

"The Waldens are worse than the darkies, always expecting to find gold somewhere."

"Pa wants you and Will to come, anyway."

"Will won't dig. Pa ought to know that by this time. Will's always restless when he is away from here."

"Pa has his head set on you and Will coming over there, anyway. You know how he is."

"We can't go tonight. Will isn't here, and I don't know when he'll come back."

"Tomorrow is soon enough. We'll spend the night. Pluto can sleep with Will, and I'll sleep with you."

Pluto started to protest that he had to get back to Marion that night, but neither of them noticed him.

"You're welcome to stay," Rosamond said, "but the bed isn't big enough for Will and Pluto. One of them will have to sleep on the floor."

"Pluto can," Darling Jill said. "Just give Pluto a pillow and a quilt and let him make himself a pallet in the hall. He won't mind."

Rosamond got up and fixed her hair and powdered her face. She looked better after that.

"I don't know when Will is coming home. Maybe not at all tonight. Sometimes he doesn't."

"He'll get sober when he goes back with us and digs a day or two. Pa will keep him sober, too."

All of them turned and listened. There was a noise on the front porch, followed by the sound of someone banging on the door.

"That's him now," Rosamond said. "He's still drunk, too. I can tell."

They waited in the room while he came through the hall and appeared at the door.

"Well, for God's sake!" Will said. "You back again?"

He stared at Darling Jill for several moments and started towards her, his hands leading him. She sidestepped, and he went on into the wall.

"Will!" Rosamond said.

"And there's old Pluto, too! How's everything out there around Marion these days?"

Pluto got up and tried to shake hands with Will, but Will started sideways toward the other side of the room.

Will sat down in the corner against the wall and placed his head on his arms. He was quiet for such a long time that all of them thought he had gone to sleep. They were getting ready to tiptoe out of the room, and they had got as far as the door when Will looked up and called them back.

"Trying to slip off from me again, weren't you? Come back here, all of you, and keep me company."

Rosamond made a gesture of helplessness and sank wearily upon the bed. Pluto and Darling Jill laughed at Will and sat down.

"How's Griselda?" Will asked. "Is that girl as good-looking as ever? What part of the country did she come from? I'd like to go there some day and take my pick."

"Please, Will," Rosamond said.

"I'm going to get that girl yet," Will said determinedly, shaking his head from side to side. "I've been wanting her for a long time now, and I can't wait much more for her, either. I'm going to get her."

"Please shut your mouth, Will," Rosamond said.

He appeared not to have heard her.

"Tell me how Griselda's looking these days, Darling Jill. Does she still look ripe for picking? I'm going to get her, so help me God! I've had my eye on her ever since she moved in the house over there. Griselda's got the sweetest pair——"

"Will!" Rosamond said.

"Aw, what the hell is the matter with you," Will said irritatedly. "It's all in the family, ain't it? Why in the hell should you bawl me out for talking about her? Buck wouldn't care much if I did get her. He can't use her all the time. Nobody ought to howl about just one tiny little bit when nobody is getting hurt. You act like I was getting ready to run down the King of England's daughter."

"Please don't talk about it now, then," Rosamond begged.

"Now, listen to me," Will said. "Griselda can't keep from being the prettiest girl in the country, no more than I can keep from wanting to get her. So what the hell does that make you? I promised myself a piece when I saw her the first time over there in Georgia, and I'll be damned if I'm going to break my own promise. You get all you bargained for. I can't help it if you raise a howl, either."

"I'll talk about it some other time, Will, if you promise to stop talking now. Try to remember who's here."

"It's all in the family, ain't it? So, what the hell!"

Darling Jill looked at Pluto and laughed. Pluto felt the blood coming over his face again, and he turned his head toward the wall where the light would shadow it. Darling Jill burst out laughing again.

There was no use in any of them trying to talk as long as Will was there.

Rosamond suddenly began to cry.

"There ain't a bit of sense in taking on like that," Will said doggedly. "It's all in the family, ain't it? Well, what the hell! Old Pluto, there, is having a good time with Darling Jill, or would if he could, and I reckon I take you plenty of times, except when you get uppity and start talking about the God damn sacredness of approaching a female, or some such talk. So, why in hell can't I talk about getting Griselda if I want to? You can't expect a girl like Griselda to put a plug in herself. Why, that would be a God damn shame! It would be a heathen sin. I swear it would. That'd be the damnedest shame I ever heard about!"

He began to cry at the thought of it. He stood up and the tears ran down his face and he sounded as if his heart were breaking. He tried to stop the flow of tears by twisting his fists into his eyesockets, but the tears fell as heavily as ever.

Rosamond got up off the bed.

"I'm glad that's over with," she said, sighing. "He'll be all right now. Just leave him alone for a little while, and he'll be himself again. Come on into the other room. I'll turn the light out so it won't hurt his eyes."

Pluto and Darling Jill followed her, leaving Will crying in the corner.

When they had all found chairs in the other room, Rosamond turned to Pluto.

"I'm awfully ashamed of what happened in the next room, Pluto," she said. "Please try to forget it and not think of it again. When Will gets drunk, he doesn't know what he's saying. He didn't mean a word of it. I'm sure of that. I wouldn't have let him embarrass you for anything, if I could have helped it. Please forget all about what he said."

"Oh, that's all right, Rosamond," he said, blushing a little. "I don't hold anything against you or Will."

"Well, I don't suppose you would," Darling Jill broke in. "It's none of your business, anyway. Just sit tight, Pluto, and keep your mouth shut."

She and Rosamond began talking about something else then, and Pluto was unable to follow the conversation. He was almost on the other side of the room from them, and their voices were lowered. He sat uncomfortably in the little chair, wishing he could sit on the floor where he would have a wider seat.

Presently Will came to the door. His face was drawn, but he showed little indication of his drinking. Apparently he had sobered.

"Glad to see you, Pluto," he said, going over and shaking hands. "It's been a long time since I've seen you. It's been nearly a year, hasn't it?"

"I reckon it has, Will."

Will drew up a chair and sat down, leaning back to look at Pluto.

"What are you doing now, the same thing as usual?"

"Well, I'm a candidate for sheriff this year," Pluto told him. "I'm running for office."

"You'll make a humdinger," Will said. "It takes a big man to hold the office of sheriff. Why that is, I don't know, but it seems to be a fact. I don't remember ever seeing a skinny sheriff."

Pluto laughed good-naturedly. He went to the window and spat tobacco juice on the ground.

"I ought to be back home now," he said, "but I'm glad to have the chance of coming over here to see you and Rosamond. I've got to get back the first thing in the morning though, and do some canvassing. I didn't get a thing done all day. I reckon I started early enough, but I only got as far as the Waldens, and now here I am over here in Carolina."

"Are the old man and the boys still digging holes in the ground over there?"

"Night and day, almost. But they're going to get an albino from the swamps to divine it for them. That's where they are tonight. They left a little before we did."

Will laughed, slapping his legs with his broad hands.

"Conjur stuff now, huh? Well, I'll be damned. I didn't know Ty Ty Walden would start using conjur, old as he is. He's always been trying to tell me how scientific he is about digging for gold. And now he's using conjur stuff! I'll be a suck-egg mule!"

Pluto wished to make a defense of some kind, but Will was laughing so much he was afraid to bring it up.

"That might help some, at that," Will continued. "And then again it mightn't. The old man ought to know, though; he's been fooling around that farm digging for gold nearly fifteen years now, and he ought to be an expert at it by this time. Reckon there's gold in that ground, sure enough, Pluto?"

"I'd hate to say," Pluto replied, "but I reckon there must be, because people have been picking up nuggets all over the country around there ever since I can remember. There's gold somewhere around there, because I've seen the nuggets."

"Every time I hear about Ty Ty digging those holes I sort of get the fever myself," Will said. "But just take me over there and put me out in that hot sun, and I lose all interest in it. I wouldn't mind striking gold there, and that's no lie. Looks like there isn't much use of waiting around here to make a living in the mill. That is, unless we do something about it."

Will had turned and was pointing out the window towards the darkened cotton mill. There was no light in the huge building, but arc lights under the trees threw a thin coating of yellow glow over the ivy-covered walls.

"When's the mill going to start up again?" Pluto asked.

"Never," Will said disgustedly. "Never. Unless we start it ourselves."

"What's the matter? Why won't it run?"

Will leaned forward in his chair.

"We're going in there some day ourselves and turn the power on," he said slowly. "If the company doesn't start up soon, that's what we're going to do. They cut the pay down to a dollar-ten eighteen months ago, and when we raised hell about it, they shut off the power and drove us out. But they still charge rent for these God damn privies we have to live in. You know why we're going to run it ourselves now, don't you?"

"But some of the other mills in the Valley are running," Pluto said. "We passed five or six lighted mills when we drove over from Augusta tonight. Maybe they'll start this one again soon."

"Like so much hell they will, at a dollar-ten. They are running the other mills because they starved the loom-weavers into going back to work. That was before the Red Cross started passing out sacks of flour. They had to go back to work and take a dollar-ten, or starve. But, by God, we don't have to do it in Scottsville. As long as we can get a sack of flour once in a while we can hold out. And the State is giving out yeast now. Mix a cake of yeast in a glass of water and drink it, and you feel pretty good for a while. They started giving out yeast because everybody in the Valley has got pellagra these days from too much starving. The mill can't get us back until they shorten the hours, or cut out the stretchout, or go back to the old pay. I'll be damned if I work nine hours a day for a dollar-ten, when those rich sons-of-bitches who own the mill ride up and down the Valley in five thousand dollar automobiles."

Will had got warmed to the subject, and once started, he could not stop. He told Pluto something of their plans for taking over the mill from the owners and running it themselves. The mill workers in Scottsville had been out of work for a year and a half already, he said, and they were becoming desperate for food and clothing. During that length of time the workers had reached an understanding among themselves that bound every man, woman, and child in the company town to a stand not to give in to the mill. The mill had tried to evict them from their homes for nonpayment of rent, but the local had got an injunction from a judge in Aiken that restrained the mill from turning the workers out of the company houses. With that, Will said, they were prepared to stand for their demands just as long as the mill stood in Scottsville.

Rosamond came over to Will and placed her hand on his shoulder. She stood silently beside him until he finished. Pluto was glad she had come. He felt uneasy in Scottsville then; Will talked as though there might be violence at any minute.

"It's time to go to bed, Will," she said softly. "If we're

going back with Darling Jill and Pluto in the morning, we ought to get some sleep. It's after midnight now."

Will put his arm around her and kissed her on the lips. She lay in his arms with her eyes closed, and her fingers were interlocked with his.

"All right," he said, raising her from his lap. "I reckon it is time."

She kissed him again and went to the door. She stood there for a moment, partly turned, looking at Will.

"Come on to bed, Darling Jill," she said.

They went into the bedroom across the hall and closed the door. Pluto began taking off his tie and shirt. After he had removed them, he began to unlace his shoes. He was ready after that to lie down on the floor and go to sleep. Will brought him a pillow and a quilt and tossed them on the floor at his feet. After leaving Pluto, he went into the room across the hall and closed the door.

"Where am I going to sleep?" he asked, standing in the middle of the room and watching Darling Jill undress.

"In the other bed, Will," Rosamond said. "Now please go along, Will, and don't bother Darling Jill. She's going to sleep with me. Please don't try to start a row. It's awfully late. It's after midnight."

Without another word he opened the door and went into the adjoining room. He took off his clothes and got into bed. It was too hot to sleep in nightclothes, or even in underwear. He stretched out on the bed and closed his eyes. He still felt a little drunk, and his head was beginning to hurt behind his temples. If he had not felt so badly just then, he knew he would have got up and argued with Rosamond about sleeping in the other room.

When Darling Jill and Rosamond had undressed, Rosamond turned out the light and opened the doors of all the rooms so there would be better circulation of air. Will could hear her open the door of his room, but he was too tired and sleepy by that time to open his eyes and call her. It was nearly one o'clock before they all went to sleep, and the only sound in the house was Pluto's snoring on his pallet across the hall.

Towards morning Will woke up and went to the kitchen for a drink of water. It was cooler then, but still too hot to get under covers. He came back and looked at Pluto on the floor, watching him in the flickering street light that shone through the windows. In the other room he went to the bed and looked down at Rosamond and Darling Jill. He stood beside the bed for several minutes, wide awake, looking down at their white bodies in the dim glow of the street light on the corner. Will thought for a moment of waking Darling Jill, but he felt a little sick and his head was beginning to throb again, and he turned away and went back to his room and closed his eyes. He did not remember anything else until the sun woke him by shining in his face. It was nearly nine o'clock then, and there was not a sound in the house.

Chapter VI

WILL WAS LYING on his side, looking out the window at the yellow company house next door, when he felt something warm against his back, something that felt like a purring kitten against his bare skin. He turned over, wide awake, partly raised on his elbow.

"Well, for God's sake!" he exclaimed.

Darling Jill sat up and began teasing him. She pulled his hair and ran her hand over his face rather hard, mashing his nose.

"You wouldn't get mad at me, would you, Will?"

"Mad?" he said. "I'm tickled to death."

"Tickle me some, Will," she said.

He reached for her, and she squirmed out of his reach. He thought he had such a grip around her that she could never get away. Will lunged after her, catching her arm and pulling her back beside him. Darling Jill cuddled up in his arms, kissing his chest, while he laughed at her.

"Where's Rosamond?" he asked, suddenly remembering her.

"She's gone downtown for a box of hairpins."

"How long has she been gone?"

"Only a minute or so."

Will raised his head and tried to see over the foot of the bed.

"Where's Pluto?"

"Sitting on the front porch."

"Hell," Will said, letting his head fall upon the pillow, "he's too lazy to get up."

She cuddled closer, putting her arms securely around him. Will pressed her breast tightly in his hand.

"Don't do that so hard, Will. You hurt me."

"I'm going to hurt you more than that before I get through with you."

"Kiss me a little first, Will. I like it."

He drew her closer and kissed her. Darling Jill threw her arms around Will and pulled herself to him. When she was closer, Will kissed her more desperately.

"Take me, Will," Darling Jill begged. "Please, Will, right now."

The woman in the yellow company house next door leaned out the window and shook a dust-mop, striking it several times against the side of the building to shake loose the sand and lint.

"Take me, Will—I can't wait," she said.

"You and me both," said he.

Will got on his hands and knees and raised Darling Jill's head until he could draw her hair from under her. He lowered her pillow, and her long brown hair hung over the bed and almost touched the floor. He looked down and saw that she had raised herself until she was almost touching him.

He awoke to hear Darling Jill screaming in his ear. He did not know how long she had been screaming. He had been oblivious to everything in the complete joy of the moment.

He raised his head after a while and looked into her face. She opened her eyes wide and smiled at him.

"That was wonderful, Will," she whispered. "Do it to me again."

He tried to free himself and arise, but she would not let him move. He knew she was waiting for him to answer her.

"Will, do it to me again."

"Damn it, Darling Jill, I can't right now."

He struggled once more to free himself and arise. She held him determinedly.

"When we get back to Georgia?"

"If it's as good in Georgia as it is in Carolina, you're damn right, Darling Jill."

"It's better in Georgia," she smiled.

"Strike me down," he said.

"I said, it's better in Georgia, Will."

"It had better be. If it's not, I'm going to bring you back to Carolina right away."

"But I would still be a Georgia girl, even if you did bring me back over here."

"All right, you win," he said, "but if all the Georgia girls are as good as you are, I'm going to stay over there."

Darling Jill raised her arm and rubbed the teethmarks where he had bitten her. Will wished he could get up and lie on his back, but she still refused to release him. He lay quietly for a while, with his eyes closed, feeling good all over.

Suddenly, like a stroke of lightning out of a cloudless sky, something hit him an awful whack on the buttocks. Will let out a yell and turned completely over in the air, falling on his back with his eyes almost popping out. He knew a bolt of lightning could not have frightened him any more thoroughly.

Before he could say anything, his eyes fell upon Rosamond at the side of the bed. She had the hairbrush raised threateningly in one hand, and with the other she was trying with all her might to turn Darling Jill over on her stomach. She succeeded in getting her sister turned over, and she whacked five or six times in quick succession, striking before Darling Jill could squirm out of reach.

Will realized that there was no sense in his attempting to get up, so he lay still, watching the hairbrush in Rosamond's hands and praying that she would not turn him over on his stomach and blister him again.

Darling Jill first laughed, but she was so badly blistered, and the blisters hurt so much, she started to cry. Will put his hand under himself and felt the big welt that had been raised on his body. He rubbed it, trying to make the stinging feeling leave. Darling Jill's buttocks were as red as fire all over, and there were ridges of scarlet welts on her tender flesh. He looked again and saw that there were welts on top of welts, rising like oblong blocks the size and shape of Rosamond's hairbrush.

Pluto stood behind Rosamond looking pityingly at Darling Jill's trembling bare body and at her quivering blistered buttocks.

"Jesus," Will said, touching the blister behind.

"Is that all you got to say for yourself?" Rosamond asked him. "I went down the street to the store and was gone for fifteen or twenty minutes. And this is what you were doing while I was away! What do you suppose Pluto would say if he could talk? Don't you know he hopes to marry her? It's almost breaking his heart to see this. Suppose you had gone downtown and had come back and found me in bed with Pluto—what would you do about it? Can't you say anything but 'Jesus'?"

Darling Jill suddenly burst out laughing. She looked at Rosamond a moment, and at Pluto. She laughed louder.

"Not with that belly, Rosamond," Darling Jill said. "How could he with that belly of his?"

Rosamond choked back a smile, but Pluto's face became crimson. He turned his head, backing against the wall and trying to press himself into it out of sight. Darling Jill put her hand on the blisters and began crying again.

"Now, wait a minute, Rosamond," Will said.

Rosamond looked down at Will, resting the hand that held the hairbrush on the foot of the bed.

"I have to beg you to sleep with me sometimes, but Darling Jill comes to the house just for one night and you take her. She's no better-looking than I am, Will."

He could think of nothing to say. He could not think of a single word to utter in reply. She continued looking down at him, however; he knew he had to say something before she would move.

"Just once was all right, wasn't it, Rosamond?"

"Once! That's all you ever say. Every time I ask you why you did it, you say you only did it once. You've had every girl in town, once. It might just as well be a hundred times. Don't you ever stop to think how it makes me feel—you out somewhere with a girl you have no business being with, and here I am sitting at home wondering where you are and what you're doing?"

Will turned his head just enough to see Darling Jill out of the corners of his eyes.

"Maybe it's because she's a Georgia girl, Rosamond. I reckon that's why."

"That's no excuse—you can't even make one up. I'm a Georgia girl myself—at least I used to be before I married you and came over here to Carolina."

Will looked at Pluto, but Pluto apparently had no suggestion worth the offer. He stared back blankly at Will.

"Rosamond, honey," he said meekly. "I felt of her and kissed her some and then the first thing I knew about it was that I just had to do it. I didn't mean any harm. That's just how it was."

"If I had a baseball bat, I'd do a thing or two to you," Rosamond replied.

Will began to have a little more confidence in his ability to argue with Rosamond. He was not afraid of Rosamond any longer, and he knew he could take the hairbrush away from her if she tried to blister him again.

"Now, listen here, Rosamond," he said. "A girl like Darling

Jill can't come around without someone getting her. She was made that way from the start."

Rosamond made as if to take the hairbrush and blister them both all over again, but she turned instead and ran to the dresser near the corner where Pluto was. She jerked open the top drawer and pulled out the little pearl-handled thirty-two she kept there. She ran back to the bed, holding it out in front of her.

"For God's sake, Rosamond," Will shouted, "Rosamond, honey, don't do that!"

Darling Jill looked up from the pillow just in time to see the hammer go back and to hear it cock. Will sat up in bed, hugging the pillow in front of him.

"If I blister you, you won't stay blistered, but if I shoot you, you'll stay shot, Will Thompson."

"Honey," he begged, "if you'll put that down, I'll never do it again. I swear to God I won't, honey. If a girl tries to make me, I'll throw her in Horse Creek. I swear to God I'll never do it again as long as I live, Rosamond, honey."

Rosamond pulled the trigger and the room was full of white smoke. She had shot at Will's feet, but she had missed. Will jumped at Rosamond, with one hand out after the little revolver. Rosamond shot it again. The bullet went between his legs, and he was scared to death. He looked down to see if he had been shot, but he was afraid to take the time to look closely. He ran to the window and jumped out, landing on his hands and chest. He was up and out of sight around the corner of the house a second after he had struck the ground.

The woman in the yellow company house next door ran to the window and stuck out her head. She saw Will running naked across the front yard and down the street as fast as his heels would fly. After he had passed from sight, she turned and looked at Rosamond at the window with the little pearl-handled revolver shaking in her hand.

"Is that Will Thompson?" the woman asked.

Rosamond leaned out the window, looking up the street and down it.

"Where did he go?" Rosamond asked her.

"Down the street yonder," the woman said, unable to keep from laughing any longer. "It's something new for Will Thompson to get shot out of his own house, ain't it? I'll have to tell Charlie about Will when he comes home. He'll die laughing when he hears about it. And Will Thompson was as naked as a jay-bird, too. Ain't that something, though?"

Rosamond went back and put the revolver into the dresser

drawer and shut it. Then she sat down in a chair and cried.

Pluto did not know what to do. He did not know whether to go after Will and try to bring him back home, or whether to stay in the room and try to quiet Rosamond and Darling Jill. Darling Jill had quieted down some, and she was not crying so loudly then. But Rosamond was. Pluto leaned over and put his hand on her arm and patted it. Rosamond threw his hand off and cried even more hysterically. Pluto decided then that the best thing for him to do was to do nothing for a while. He sat down again and waited.

Presently Rosamond got up and ran to the bed where her sister was. She threw herself upon the bed, hugging Darling Jill in her arms and bursting into tears once more. They both lay there consoling one another. Pluto looked on uneasily. He had expected to see them fly at each other, pulling hair, scratching, and calling each other names. But they were doing nothing of the sort. They were actually hugging one another and weeping together. Pluto could not understand why Rosamond did not try to shoot Darling Jill, or at least why she was not angry with her. To look at them at that moment, Pluto could not imagine how Rosamond had acted as she had a few minutes before. They were behaving as though suffering a common bereavement.

When Rosamond's sobs had almost ceased, she sat up and looked down at her sister. The red welts on Darling Jill's buttocks still throbbed with intense pain, and she could not lie upon them. Rosamond touched one of the welts tenderly with the tips of her fingers as though she might be able to soothe the hurt a little thereby.

"Lie where you are until I come back," Rosamond told her. "I'll only be gone a moment."

She ran to the kitchen and came back with a cup of lard and a large bath towel. She sat down on the side of the bed and dipped her fingers into the grease.

"Come here, Pluto," she said, not turning around to look at him. "You can help me."

Pluto came over to the bed, blushing to the tips of his ears at the sight of Darling Jill lying naked before him.

"Lift her gently, Pluto, and hold her across your lap," Rosamond instructed. "Now be careful. Don't irritate those welts, whatever you do."

Pluto put his arms under Darling Jill, laying the palms of his hands flat against her breasts and thighs. He jerked his hands from under her, his face and neck burning.

"Now, what's the matter?"

"Maybe you had better lift her."

"Don't be silly, Pluto. How can I? I'm not strong."

He put his hands under her again, closing his eyes and compressing his lips.

"Hurry, Pluto, and let me put this lard on those swollen places before they turn blue."

Pluto lifted her and turned around. He sat down on the side of the bed next to Rosamond with Darling Jill lying across his knees. Rosamond began applying the lard at once. Pluto would have watched her, but he could not take his eyes from Darling Jill's long brown hair hanging to the floor. He raised her a little so her hair would not touch it. She winced once or twice when Rosamond touched her, but she did not protest or try to get up. When the lard had been carefully spread, Rosamond wiped her fingers on a piece of cloth and began folding the towel until it was a long thick bandage. Pluto looked down at Darling Jill's soft buttocks with a sudden desire to touch them and try to soothe the pain. Each time he looked down at her in his lap, though, he began to blush all over again.

"Help her to her feet, Pluto," Rosamond said. "Lift her up and let her stand on her feet, Pluto."

Darling Jill stood up in front of Pluto and her sister while the towel was being fastened securely around her. Pluto's gaze was fixed on a point of her body that happened to be the closest. He looked straight ahead, moving his eyes neither to the right nor to the left. He knew Darling Jill was looking down at him, but he could not bring himself to raise his head and look up into her face.

He was not at all certain, but he believed she had leaned forward towards him.

"Like me, Pluto?" Darling Jill asked, smiling.

Pluto's face trembled, his neck stung with a sudden rush of blood, and he tried to look up and meet her eyes. It was an exertion for him to move his head upward and backward, but he forced himself to move it.

"I'm going to be angry if you won't say you like me now," she pouted.

"I'm crazy about you, Darling Jill," he said, partly choked. "And that's a fact."

"Why do you turn red in the face and neck when you see me like this, Pluto?"

He felt fresh blood rush in to embarrass him. He pulled at a loose thread in the counterpane without knowing what he was doing.

"I like it, though," he replied.

"Marry me, Pluto?"

"Right now, or anytime you say," he told her. "And that's a fact."

"But your belly is too big, Pluto."

"Aw, now, Darling Jill, don't let that stand in the way."

"If it wasn't so big, Pluto, you could stand closer."

"Aw, now, Darling Jill."

"And that's a fact," she said, mocking him.

"Aw, now, Darling Jill," he said, reaching out to put his arms around her waist.

She allowed him to draw her close enough to be kissed. Pluto drew her between his legs and stretched his head as high as he could but her lips were so far above his reach he knew he could never kiss her unless he stood up beside her or unless she bent down to him. He reasoned that it would be much easier for her to bend over than it would be for him to get to his feet, and he knew she was aware of it. But she remained standing erectly in his arms, tantalizing him by refusing to bend over and place her lips on his. When he did not know what to do, unless it was to get to his feet beside her, Darling Jill leaned against him and twisted her body a little. Before he realized how it had come about, he felt her warm breast against his face and he was kissing her madly.

"Stop it this instant, Darling Jill!" Rosamond said, getting up and pulling them apart. "Stop teasing Pluto like that. It's a shame to treat the poor boy the way you do all the time. Some of these days he's going to turn on you, and anything may happen."

Darling Jill, jerking herself out of his embrace, ran to the door and into the next room holding the towel around her buttocks. Pluto sat in a daze, his hands lifeless beside him, and his mouth hanging agape. Rosamond, turning, saw him; she felt so sorry for him that she came back and patted his cheek tenderly.

Chapter VII

AT NOON THE WHISTLES of the cotton mills up and down the Valley blew for the midday shutdown. Everywhere else there was a sudden cessation of vibration, and the men and women came out of the buildings taking cotton from their ears.

In the company town of Scottsville the people did not move from the chairs on their porches. It was noon, and it was dinner-time; but in Scottsville the people sat with contracted bellies and waited for the end of the strike.

The woman in the yellow company house next door made a fire in the cook-stove and put on a pan of water to boil. Such as there was to eat, she and her husband and the children would devour without breaking the tightly drawn lines at the corners of their mouths. Each successive day was a victory; for eighteen months they had stood out against the mill, and they would never give in while there was hope.

Rosamond suggested making a freezer of ice cream. "Will would like some when he comes back," she said.

Pluto was sent down the street for a cake of ice. He went to the store at the corner, hurrying down and back as fast as he could walk, while Rosamond was scalding the freezer and paring the peaches. He was frightened every second he was in the Valley. He was afraid somebody would jump at him from behind a tree and slash his throat from ear to ear, and even in the house he was afraid to sit with his back to a door or window.

Darling Jill came out on the back porch while Rosamond was preparing the cream and sat down on a pillow in the shade. She had combed her hair but had not pinned it up. It hung down her back, covering her shoulders, and reached almost to the floor. Rosamond had lent her a dressing gown, and she wore that over the towel and the black silk stockings supported by canary yellow garters.

When Pluto returned with the cake of ice, the cream was ready to be frozen. He saw that it was up to him to turn the freezer.

It was cool on the shaded back porch, now that the sun was passing over the house. There was a breeze that blew occasionally, and the ninety-degree temperature at midday was bearable. Broad, green, cool Horse Creek looked like an oblong lake down below, stretching for miles up and down the Valley.

"I've got to be getting home," Pluto said. "And that's a fact."

"The voters won't miss you," Darling Jill told him. "They'll be glad you're not there today to worry them. Anyway, we're not ready to go back yet."

"I missed yesterday, and the day before, and two or three days before that. And now I'm missing today, too."

"When we get back, I'll campaign some for you, Pluto," Darling Jill said. "I'll get more votes than you will know what to do with."

"I wish I was back now, anyway," he said. "And that's a fact."

He turned the freezer faster, hoping to finish it in time to start back within the hour.

"I wish Will would come back," Rosamond said. "Do you suppose he'll stay away this time—and never come home?"

Darling Jill sighed and looked into the kitchen window of the yellow company house next door. The people over there were eating sandwiches and drinking iced tea. It made Darling Jill a little hungry to watch them eat.

Rosamond thought the cream was getting stiff. Pluto was having difficulty in turning the freezer at the pace he had started, and the perspiration rolled from his face and his mouth hung open with exhaustion. He held the freezer with one hand and turned doggedly with the other.

No one happened to be looking in that direction when Will stuck his head around the corner of the house and watched them for several minutes. When he saw that Pluto was freezing ice cream, he stepped around the corner and walked slowly down the path to the steps.

"Why, there's Will now," Darling Jill said, seeing him first.

Will stopped in his tracks and looked at Rosamond.

"Will!" she cried.

She jumped up and ran down the steps to meet him, throwing her arms around his neck and kissing him frantically.

"Will, are you all right?"

He patted her shoulder and kissed her. He was wearing only a pair of khaki pants he had borrowed somewhere, and he was barefooted and shirtless.

Rosamond drew him up the steps and made him sit down in her chair. Pluto stopped turning the crank to look at him. He had not expected to see Will again for a long time.

"The cream is stiff by this time, Pluto," Rosamond said. "Take off the top while we're getting the dishes and spoons. And be careful of the salt. Take out some of the ice before you forget it."

She was gone only a moment. Darling Jill took the large spoon and filled the dishes, and passed them around. Rosamond remained with Will, refusing to leave him again. He took a bite of the peach ice cream and smiled at her.

"Did you hear anything about the mill opening?" she asked
him.

"No," he replied.

The women in the yellow company houses asked that every
day, but the men always said they had heard nothing.

"The other mills are still running, aren't they?"

"I reckon so," he said.

"When will ours start up?"

"I don't know."

The thought of the other mills operating regularly stiffened
Will. He sat up erectly and stared down at the broad green
water. Horse Creek lay down there as calm as a smooth lake.
The thought of the other mills in the Valley running night
and day started a vivid picture that began to unroll across
his eyes. He could see the ivy-walled cotton mill beside the
green water. It was early morning, and the whistle blew, calling eager girls to work. They were never men, the people who
entered the mill now; the mill wished to employ girls, because
girls never rebelled against the harder work, the stretching-
out, the longer hours, or the cutting of pay. Will could see
the girls running to the mill in the early morning while the
men stood in the streets looking, but helpless.

All day long there was a quiet stillness about the ivy-
walled mill. The machinery did not hum so loudly when the
girls operated it. The men made the mill hum with noise when
they worked there. But when evening came, the doors were
flung open and the girls ran out screaming in laughter. When
they reached the street, they ran back to the ivy-covered walls
and pressed their bodies against it and touched it with their
lips. The men who had been standing idly before it all day
long came and dragged them home and beat them unmerci-
fully for their infidelity.

Will woke up with a start to see Pluto and Rosamond and
Darling Jill. He had been away, and when he returned, he
was surprised to see them there. He rubbed his eyes and wondered if he had been asleep. He knew he had not been, though,
because his dish was empty. It lay in his hands heavy and
hard.

"Christ," he murmured.

He remembered the time when the mill down below was
running night and day. The men who worked in the mill
looked tired and worn, but the girls were in love with the
looms and the spindles and the flying lint. The wide-eyed
girls on the inside of the ivy-walled mill looked like potted
plants in bloom.

Up and down the Valley lay the company towns and the ivy-walled cotton mills and the firm-bodied girls with eyes like morning-glories and the men stood on the hot streets looking at each other while they spat their lungs into the deep yellow dust of Carolina. He knew he could never get away from the blue-lighted mills at night and the bloody-lipped men on the streets and the unrest of the company towns. Nothing could drag him away from there now. He might go away and stay a while, but he would be restless and unhappy until he could return. He had to stay there and help his friends find some means of living. The mill streets could not exist without him; he had to stay and walk on them and watch the sun set on the mill at night and rise on it in the morning. In the mill streets of the Valley towns the breasts of girls were firm and erect. The cloth they wove under the blue lights clothed their bodies, but beneath the covering the motions of erect breasts were like the quick movements of hands in unrest. In the Valley towns beauty was begging, and the hunger of strong men was like the whimpering of beaten women.

"Jesus Christ," he murmured under his breath.

He looked up to find Darling Jill filling his empty dish with peach-flecked ice cream. Before she could turn and go away, Will grabbed her arm and pulled her to him. He kissed her cheek several times, squeezing her hand tightly.

"For God's sake don't ever come over here and work in a mill," he begged. "You wouldn't do that, would you, Darling Jill?"

She started to laugh, but when she saw his face, she became anxious.

"What's the matter, Will? Are you sick?"

"Oh, nothing is the matter," he said, "but for God's sake don't ever go to work in a cotton mill."

Rosamond laid her hand on his and urged him to eat the cream before it melted.

He closed his eyes and saw the yellow company houses stretched endlessly through Scottsville. In the rear of the houses he saw tight-lipped women sitting at kitchen windows with their backs to the cold cook-stoves. In the streets in front of the houses he saw the bloody-lipped men spitting their lungs into the yellow dust. As far as he could see, there were rows of ivy-walled mills beside broad cool Horse Creek, and in them the girls sang, drowning out the sound of moving machinery. The spinning mills and the fabric mills and the bleacheries were endless, and the eager girls with erect breasts and eyes like morning-glories ran in and out endlessly.

"Pluto is going to take us over to Georgia," Rosamond said softly. "You'll have a good rest over there at home, Will. You'll feel lots better when we come back."

He was glad then that they were going to Ty Ty's for a while, but he hated to go away and leave the others there to sit and wait and stand out against the mill. When he got back, he would feel much better, though; perhaps they could then break open the steel-barred doors of the mill and turn on the power. He would like to come back to the Valley and stand in the mill and hear the hum of machinery, even if there was to be no cloth woven any time soon.

"All right," he said. "When do we start, Pluto?"

"I'm ready now," Pluto said. "I'd like to get back in time to count some votes before supper."

Rosamond and Darling Jill went into the house to dress. Will and Pluto sat looking down at the green water below. It looked cool, and it did make the breeze feel cooler after passing over it. But the temperature was even under the cloudless sky. The grass and weeds wilted in the sun, and the dust that blew down from the cultivated uplands settled on the ground and on the buildings like powdered paint.

Will went inside to take off the khaki pants and put on his own clothes.

They were ready to start and had locked the house when Will saw someone coming up the street.

"Where you going, Will?" the man asked, stopping and looking at them and at Pluto's car.

"Just over to Georgia for a day or two, Harry."

Will felt like a traitor, running off like that. He waited for Rosamond to go down the walk first.

"Are you sure you're not leaving for good, Will?" the man asked suspiciously.

"I'll be back in town in a few days, Harry. And when I get back, you'll know it."

"All right, but don't forget to come back. If everybody leaves, pretty soon the company is going to rush a crew of operators in here and start up without us. We've all got to stay here and hold out. If the mill ever once got started without us, we wouldn't have a chance in the world. You know that, Will."

Will went down the walk and got in front of Rosamond. He walked down the street with the other man, talking to him in a low voice. They stopped several yards away and began arguing. Will would talk a little while, tapping the other man on the chest with his forefinger; the other man would nod his head and glance down at the ivy-walled mill below. They turned and walked a little further, both talking at the same time. When they stopped again, the other man began talking to Will, tapping him on the chest with his forefinger. Will nodded his head, shook it violently, nodded again.

"We can't let anybody go in there and wreck the machinery," Will said. "Nobody wants to see that done."

"That's just what I've been trying to tell you, Will. What we want to do is to go in there and turn the power on. When the company comes and sees what's happening, they'll either try to drive us out, or else get down to business."

"Now listen, Harry," Will said, "when that power is turned on, nobody on God's earth is going to shut it off. It's going to stay turned on. If they try to turn it off, then we'll—well, God damn it, Harry, the power is going to stay turned on."

"I've always been in favor of turning it on and never shutting it off. That's what I've tried to tell the local, but what can you tell that son-of-a-bitch A.F.L.? Nothing! They're drawing pay to keep us from working. When we start to work, the money will stop coming in here to pay them. Well, God damn it, Will, we're nothing but suckers to listen to them talk about arbitration. Let the mill run three shifts, maybe four shifts, when we turn the power on, but keep it running all the time. We can turn out as much print cloth as the company can, maybe a lot more. But all of us will be working then, anyway. We can speed up after everybody gets back on the job. What we're after now is turning on the power. And if they try to shut off the power, then we'll get in there and—well, God damn it, Will, the power ain't going to be shut off once we turn it on. Now, God damn it, Will, I've never been in favor of wrecking anything. You know that, and so does everybody else. That son-of-a-bitch A.F.L. started that talk when they heard we were thinking about turning the power on. All I'm after is running the mill."

"That's what I've been saying at every local meeting since the shutdown," Will said. "The local is all hooped-up with the A.F.L. They've been saying nothing is going to get us our jobs back except arbitrating. I've never been in favor of that. You can't talk to the company and get nothing but a one-sided answer. They're not going to say a thing but 'a dollar-ten.' You know that as well as I do. And how in the hell can a man pay rent on these stinking privies we live in out of a dollar-ten? You tell me how it can be done, and I'll be the first to vote for arbitrating. No, Sir. It just can't be done."

"Well, I'm in favor of going in there and turning on the power. That's what I've been saying all the time. I've never said anything else, and I never will."

Rosamond came part of the way and called Will. He turned away from the other man and asked what she wanted. He had forgotten all about the trip to Georgia.

"Come on, Will," she said. "Pluto is all up in the air about waiting so long to start. He's running for sheriff back home, and he's got to canvass for votes. You and Harry can finish that argument when we come back in a day or two."

He and Harry talked for several moments, and Will turned and followed Rosamond to the car. Darling Jill was in the driver's seat, with Pluto beside her. Will sat down on the back seat with Rosamond. The motor had been idling for five minutes or longer while they waited.

Will leaned out of the car to wave to Harry.

"Try to get that meeting called for Friday night," he shouted. "By God, we'll show the A.F.L. and the company what we mean by turning the power on."

Darling Jill raced down the unpaved street and turned the corner recklessly. They were off in a cloud of dust that blew up and sifted thickly through the hot air to settle on the trees and front porches of the yellow company houses.

They sped along the hot concrete toward Augusta, passing an almost endless cluster of company houses. They passed through the other company towns, slowing down in the restricted zones and looking out at the humming mills. They could see the men and girls through the open windows and they could almost hear the hum of the moving machinery behind the ivy-covered walls. Along the streets there were few people to be seen. There were not nearly so many as there were on the streets of Scottsville.

"Hurry up and let's get to Augusta," Will said. "I want to get out of the Valley as soon as this car can take me out. I'm damn tired of looking at spinning mills and company houses every minute of the day and night."

He knew he was not tired of looking at them, or of living with them; it was the sight of so many open mills that irritated him.

Graniteville, Warrenville, Langley, Bath, and Clearwater were left behind, and out of the Valley they raced over the hot concrete at seventy miles an hour. When they got to the top of Schultz Hill, they could look down over the dead city of Hamburg and see the muddy Savannah and, on the Georgia side, the wide flood plain on which Augusta was built. Up above it was The Hill, clustered with skyscraping resort hotels and three-story white residences.

While coasting down the long hill toward the Fifth Street Bridge, Rosamond said something about Jim Leslie.

"He lives in one of those fine houses on The Hill," Will said. "Why doesn't the son-of-a-bitch ever come to see us?"

"Jim Leslie would come, if it wasn't for his wife," Rosamond said. "Gussie thinks she's too good to speak to us. She makes Jim Leslie call us lint-heads."

"I'd rather be a God-forsaken lint-head and live in a yellow company house than be what she and Jim Leslie are. I've seen him on Broad Street and when I spoke to him, he'd turn around and run off so people wouldn't see him talking to me."

"Jim Leslie didn't use to be that way," Rosamond said. "When he was a boy at home, he was just like all the rest of us. He married a society girl on The Hill, though, when he made a lot of money, and now he won't have anything to do with us. He was a little different from the rest of us at the start, though. There was something about him—I don't know what it was."

"Jim Leslie is a cotton broker," Will said. "He got rich gambling on cotton futures. He didn't make the money he's got—he crooked it. You know what a cotton broker is, don't you? Do you know why they're called brokers?"

"Why?"

"Because they keep the farmers broke all the time. They lend a little money, and then they take the whole damn crop. Or else they suck the blood out of a man by running the price up and down forcing him to sell. That's why they call them cotton brokers. And that's what Jim Leslie Walden is. If he was my brother, I'd treat him just like I would treat a scab in Scottsville."

Chapter VIII

IT WAS NOT QUITE DARK, but the stars were beginning to come out, and lights in the houses beside the road blinked in the late twilight. When they were half a mile from home, they could see moving lights that looked as if lanterns were being carried by moving men.

There was a stir and a hum about the place that showed that something was going on. Darling Jill speeded up the car to find out what it was. She slowed down at the turn, burning the brake bands until the odor of rubber enveloped them in the dust.

Ty Ty came running around the house holding out a smoking lantern in front of him. His face was red with the day's heat, and his clothes were caked with dried clay that clung to the cloth like beggar-lice. They all jumped out to meet him.

"What's the matter, Pa?" Rosamond asked him excitedly.

"Great guns," he said, "we're digging like all get-out. We've sunk a hole twenty feet since this morning, and I don't mean maybe, either. We've been doing the fastest digging in ten years."

He pulled at them, urging them to follow him. He broke into a run, leading them across the yard and around the corner of the house. Stopping abruptly, they found themselves balanced on the rim of a lantern-lit crater at the side of the house. Down on the floor of it, Shaw and Buck and Black Sam were digging into the clay. On the other side of the crater, opposite them, was Uncle Felix with another smoking lantern and a shot gun. There was another man beside him, looking like a ghost in the flickering light.

"Who's that over there?" Will asked.

Ty Ty shouted down at Buck and Shaw. Griselda came suddenly into view, emerging from somewhere in the darkness.

"Boys," Ty Ty shouted, "we've been working since early this morning, and I reckon we'd better stop and rest some. Will's here now, and we'll all start in again tomorrow morning bright and early. Come on up and see the folks."

Buck threw down his shovel, but Shaw kept on picking away at the hard clay. Buck began arguing with him, trying to get him to stop for the night and rest. Black Sam was already climbing out of the hole.

Griselda and Darling Jill went into the house and lit the lamps.

"I'm hungry as all get-out, girls," Ty Ty said.

Uncle Felix picked up the smoking lantern at his feet, poking the other man with the end of the shotgun. He urged the strange man around the house towards the barn.

"Who's that?" Pluto asked. "Is he a voter?"

"That? Why, that's the all-white man you put me on the track of, Pluto. Great guns, Pluto, that's that albino we roped in the swamps."

They walked around the house behind the man and Uncle Felix. The colored man was urging him forward, talking to him while he poked with the end of the gun.

"I didn't tell you no lie about him, did I?" Pluto asked. "I said he was down there in the swamp, didn't I, Ty Ty?"

"You didn't tell no lie about him being there, but you sure overestimated the trouble he might cause. Why, that all-white man was no more trouble to bring home than a dead rabbit. He came along just as peaceful, Pluto. But I ain't taking no chances with him. He might be playing possum. That's why I keep Uncle Felix guard over him day and night."

"Did he divine for you, Ty Ty?"

"Just like four and four make eight," Ty Ty said. "When we got him here and told him what he was to do, why the first thing he did was to point out that spot where the new hole is now. He said that was the place to dig for the lode. And that's where it is."

"How do you know it is? Did you find any nuggets?"

"Well, not exactly. But we're getting warmer every minute."

"Can he talk?" Will asked.

"Talk? Well, I reckon he can, and then some. Why, that all-white man will talk your arm off if you give him half a showing. He can argue like nobody's business. My jaws are so tired now that they're almost locked down from talking with him. I ain't scared of him no longer, either. He's just like me and you and everybody else, Will, only he's all-white, including his hair and eyes. True, his eyes are a little pinkish, but even that passes for white when the light ain't so good."

"Did you mention to him that I am running for sheriff?" Pluto asked.

"Now, Pluto," Ty Ty said, "I ain't got no time letting him off to cast a vote. He's going to stay right where he is, day and night. We're going to dig gold out of that hole, even if we have to go clear down to China to raise it. But we're getting warm now. It ain't going to be long before we strike that lode and start shoveling out those yellow guinea eggs."

Ty Ty stopped at the barn gate.

"I'm awfully hungry now," he said. "Let's go back to the house and hurry up the girls cooking something to eat, and after supper we can bring him up to the house and let everybody take a good look and see what an albino looks like at close range."

Ty Ty turned and started back to the house. Will and Pluto

followed behind. They had wished to see the man in the barn right away, but neither of them was anxious to go there unless Ty Ty was with them.

"You ought not to have let him set you digging right beside the house," Will said. "That was the wrong thing to do, it looks like to me. The house might tumble right down into the hole."

"I've seen to that," Ty Ty said. "Me and the boys and Black Sam brace it up as we go along. We've got it propped so it can't fall in the hole. It don't matter so much if it does, though; when we strike the lode, we'll be rich enough to build any number of fine houses, lots finer than that one is."

"I don't know so much about that part," Pluto said, "but it does look like you're digging on God's little acre."

"Well, that won't worry you long," Ty Ty said. "I shifted God's little acre clear over to the back side of the farm this morning. There ain't no danger of us striking the lode on it for yet a while to come. God's little acre is as safe over there as it would be down in Florida."

Ty Ty and Will went into the house, but Pluto sat down on the porch where it was cooler.

Griselda and Rosamond were cooking supper, and Darling Jill was setting the table. Black Sam had brought in an armful of fat pine knots, and the cook-stove was red hot on top. Everybody was hungry, but it would not take long to boil the grits and make the sweet potatoes with the heat Black Sam had provided. Griselda had sliced half a ham and it was frying on two griddles.

Everyone forgot about Pluto. Just as Will and Ty Ty were getting up from the table, Darling Jill remembered that he had not had supper, and she ran to find him. She brought him into the dining-room protesting that he did not have time to stay. He kept on saying that he had to get out on the road and canvass the voters before bed-time that night.

"Now, Pluto," Ty Ty said, "you just sit and eat. When you finish, we're going to bring that all-white man up here from the barn and let everybody get a good look at him in the light. He has to come to eat just like the rest of us, and he can eat here just as well as he can in the barn. That'll give Uncle Felix a breathing spell, because he's been guarding him ever since we brought him back last night."

Buck and Shaw got ready to drive to Marion for some new shovels. Since beginning anew, they had broken one shovel handle, and one blade had bent. Ty Ty wished to get a new shovel for Will, and he himself thought he could dig better with a new one. Buck and Shaw washed and changed their clothes and got ready to leave.

Ty Ty took Will and Pluto into the living-room while the girls were clearing the table and stacking the dishes in the kitchen for Black Sam to wash. He was eager to tell them how the albino had been captured.

"Buck saw him first," Ty Ty began. "He's right proud of it, and I don't blame him none, either. We were down in that swamp below Marion waiting for the first sight of him when Buck said he thought he'd go up to a house just off the road and inquire about an all-white man. We drove up there in the car and stopped in the yard, and Buck got out and rapped on the porch. I was looking the other way at the time, thinking maybe I might see some signs of the albino in the distance, and I don't know what Shaw was doing. But Shaw wasn't looking the same way Buck was, because before I knew it I heard Buck yell, 'Here he is!' "

"Was he in the house, there?" Pluto asked.

"Was he?" Ty Ty said. "Well, I reckon he was. When I turned around, there he was, big as life, standing in the door looking like a man who's just been ducked in a flour barrel. He was wearing overalls and a blue work shirt, but he was white everywhere else I could see."

"Did he run?"

"Run nothing! He came out on the porch and asked Buck what we was after. Buck grabbed him around the legs, and Shaw and me jumped out on the ground with the plow-lines. We had him tied up in no time, just like you rope a calf to take to market. He yelled some, and kicked a great deal, but that didn't cut no ice with the boys and me. Then pretty soon a woman came to the door to see what all the fuss was about. She was like all women, and I mean by that, she wasn't all-white like the albino was. She said to me, 'What on earth are you folks doing?' And she said to the albino, 'What's the matter, Dave?' He didn't say anything for a while, and that's how we came to know what his name was. It's Dave. Directly he said, 'These sons-of-bitches have got me all roped up.' Then she started yelling and ran through the house and out the back door into the swamp, and that's the last I saw or heard of her. She was his wife, I reckon, but I can't see what an albino has got business of marrying for. It's a good thing we brought him away. I hate to see a white woman taking up with a coal-black darky, and this was just about as bad, because he is an all-white man."

"Now that you've got him, what can he do?" Will said.

"Do? Why, locate the lode for us, Will."

"That's not scientific, like you've always talked about being," Will said. "Now, tell the honest-to-God truth. Is it?"

"I reckon it is, if I know what I'm doing. Some folks say a well-diviner ain't a scientific man, but I maintain he is. And I stick up the same way for a gold-diviner."

"There's nothing scientific about breaking off a willow branch and walking over the ground with it looking for a stream of water underground. It's hit or miss. I've heard them say, 'Dig here,' and when the shaft had been sunk a couple of hundred feet, there wasn't a drop of water on the drill. You might just as well roll high-dice for water as to walk over the ground with a willow branch. Sure, a willow branch will dip sometimes, and other times it will rise up, too. If I was going to sink a well, I wouldn't try to divine water with a piece of willow limb. I'd roll high-dice for it before I'd make a fool out of myself doing that."

"You just haven't got a scientific mind, Will," Ty Ty said sadly. "That's the whole trouble with your talk. Now, take me. I'm scientific clear through to the marrow, and I've always been, and I reckon I'll be to the end. I don't laugh and poke fun at scientific notions like you do."

After the hearty supper of grits and sweet potatoes, hot biscuits and fried ham, both Ty Ty and Will were feeling good. Pluto had eaten as much, if not more than anyone in the house, but he was restless. He knew he ought to leave and go home so he could get up at break of day the next morning and make an early start campaigning. He was beginning to worry about the outcome of the election. If he were not elected sheriff, he did not know what he was going to do. He did not have a job, and the colored share-cropper who worked his sixty-acre farm could not make enough cotton to provide him with a living. He might be able to peddle something, if he could find some novelty that people would buy. He had been selling first one thing and then another for eight or ten years, but he had never been able to make much more than expense money for his car out of it. For one thing, he was never able to get around much. When he remained in town, he liked to sit in the big chair in the pool room and call shots, and to talk about politics. He knew he should not spend so much of his time in the pool room, but he just could not get out in the hot sun day after day trying to sell laundry bluing or furniture polish that people did not wish to buy, or if they did, not have enough money to pay for. But if he were elected sheriff, that would be another matter. He would draw a good salary, with fees in addition, and the deputies could go out and serve all the papers and make all the arrests. He could still sit in the pool room most of the time and call shots across the table.

"I reckon I'd better be going home, now," he said.

He made no effort to rise from the chair, and no one paid any attention to him.

Darling Jill came in with Griselda and Rosamond and patted Pluto's bald head. She would not come in front of him where he could put his hands on her, and he was forced to submit to her play while he hoped she would soon consent to sit on his lap.

"When are you going to bring that albino up here so we can see him?" Will asked.

"Stay calm and hold your horses a little longer," Ty Ty told him. "Black Sam has got to finish washing the dishes first, and then I'll send him down to the barn for him. Uncle Felix can eat his supper while everybody is looking at the all-white man in here."

"I'm just crazy to see him," Darling Jill said, playing with Pluto's head.

"I've got to be going home," Pluto said. "And that's a fact."

Pluto's statement was completely ignored.

"I'd like to see him, too," Rosamond said, looking at Griselda. "What does he look like?"

"He's big and strong. And good-looking too."

"Aw, hell," Will said, making a face, "ain't that just like a woman?"

"I don't aim to have no fooling around with him," Ty Ty told them. "You girls can just walk off and call crows, if that's what you've got on your minds. He's got to keep on the job for me all the time."

Darling Jill sat down on Pluto's lap. He was surprised, and pleased. He beamed with pleasure when she put her arms around his neck and kissed him.

"Why don't you and Pluto get married?" Ty Ty asked.

"I'm willing, day or night," Pluto said eagerly.

"I declare, it sure would be a big load off my mind if you would."

"I'm willing, day or night," Pluto repeated. "And that's a fact."

"You're willing for what?" Darling Jill asked.

"To get married anytime you say so."

"To me? Marry me?"

"You bet your boots," he said, jerking his head at her. "I'm crazy about you, Darling Jill, and I can't keep on waiting for it to happen. I want to get married right away."

"When you swallow that belly, I might think about it." She began pounding it with her fists, hitting him without mercy. "But I wouldn't marry you now, you horse's ass."

Not even Pluto spoke after that. There was not a word spoken for nearly a minute. Then Griselda got up and tried to make Darling Jill leave Pluto alone.

"Hush, Darling Jill," Griselda said; "don't talk like that. It isn't nice."

"Well, he is an old horse's ass, isn't he? What would you call him? A doll-baby? He looks like a horse's ass to me."

Ty Ty got up and went out of the room. Everyone supposed he was going down to the barn and bring back the albino. The others in the room sat still and tried not to look at Pluto. Pluto sat glumly alone, hurt by Darling Jill's treatment of him, but all the more eager to marry her.

Chapter IX

THERE WAS A STAMPING of heavy-shod feet on the front porch. Ty Ty's voice could be heard above the sound, however; he was telling Uncle Felix to take Dave into the house and show him off.

"Just shove him in," Ty Ty said. "The folks in there are waiting to get a look at him."

The albino was the first to appear in the door; Uncle Felix was behind him, shotgun leveled against his back, and looking scared to death. He was glad to be relieved of his responsibility, if only temporarily, when Ty Ty told him to go to the kitchen and eat his supper.

"Well, folks, here he is," Ty Ty said proudly. He laid the shotgun across the chair seat and led Dave into the room. "Take a seat and make yourself at home."

"What's your name, fellow?" Will asked him, partly dazzled by the whiteness of his skin and hair.

"Dave."

"Dave how-many?"

"Dave Dawson."

"Can you divine a lode of gold?"

"I don't know. I've never tried it before."

"Well, then," Will said, "you'd better begin praying about it, because if you can't, all these folks are going to be pretty mad at you and I don't know what might be liable to happen to you."

"Sure, he can do it," Ty Ty broke in. "He can do it and don't know it."

"I want to see the gold you divine, fellow," Will told him. "I want to feel it in my hand, and bite it."

"Now, don't get him all shy and scared, Will. When he grows up, he's going to be some almighty gold-diviner. He's young yet. Just give him time."

Darling Jill and Rosamond had been looking at the strange man without taking their eyes from him. Rosamond was a little afraid of him, and she drew back in her chair involuntarily. Darling Jill, though, leaned forward and gazed steadily into his eyes. He felt her staring at him and he looked at her. Dave bit his lip, wondering who she was. He had never seen a girl he thought so beautiful before, and he was trembling a little.

With their eyes upon him, Dave felt like an animal on exhibition. All of them were looking at him, and he could only look at one person at a time. His eyes went around the room, returning to Darling Jill. The more he saw her, the more he liked her. He wondered if she were the wife of one of the men in the room.

"How do you like it up here on solid ground, fellow?" Will asked.

"It's all right."

"But you'd rather be back home in the swamp, wouldn't you?"

"I don't know," he replied.

He looked again at Darling Jill. She was smiling at him then, and he dared to smile back at her.

"Well, I'll declare," Ty Ty said, leaning back in his chair. "Just look at him and Darling Jill carry-on, would you, folks!"

Up until then Ty Ty had not for a moment considered Dave a human being. Since the night before, Ty Ty had looked upon him as something different from a man. But it dawned upon him when he saw Darling Jill's smile that the boy was actually a person. He was still an albino, though, and he was said to possess unearthly powers to divine gold. In that respect, Ty Ty still held him above all other men.

"What would your wife say, fellow, if she saw you here making eyes at Darling Jill?" Will asked him.

"She's pretty," the boy said simply.

"Who? Your wife?"

"No," he answered quickly, looking at Darling Jill. "She is."

"I don't reckon you're the first one to say that, fellow, but she's hard to get unless she's the one who's doing the getting. There're too many after her now, to make her come easy. See that fat man over there in the corner? Well, he's after her, for one. He's been trying God-knows-how-long, but he hasn't got her yet himself. You'll have to go some to get her, fellow, I'm telling you."

Pluto looked uneasily at the tall slim boy sitting in the straight-backed chair in the center of the room. He did not like the way Darling Jill made eyes at Dave, either. That kind of a beginning brought a dangerous ending.

"It's only fair to set the boy straight at the start, seeing as how he's a male and women are females," Ty Ty said. "I've had the side of my barn kicked off just because I was careless enough to lead a stud horse into the wind when I should have led him with the wind."

"Talking don't help much," Will broke in. "If you've got a rooster, he's going to crow."

"Don't listen to him," Ty Ty continued. "I know what I'm about. Now, see that girl sitting in the middle? That's Buck's wife and her name is Griselda and, if I do say so myself, God never made a finer-looking woman in His day. But leave her alone. Then the other one, there, with the dimples is Rosamond. She's Will's wife. Leave her alone, too. And the one you're looking at is Darling Jill. She's nobody's wife yet, but that don't make her free for the asking, and I'm trying my best to make her marry Pluto. Pluto is the fat man in the corner. He's running for sheriff this year. I may let you off to vote for him when the time comes."

"It's no use telling him to leave Darling Jill alone." Will said. "It's a waste of words to say that. Just look at them make eyes at each other."

"I wasn't going to mention it, but since you brought it up, I reckon he might just as well know that I can't stop Darling Jill from what she sets her head on. She's as crazy as hell sometimes, and about nothing."

While Dave and Darling Jill were looking at each other, Ty Ty fell to talking again. His voice was not raised, but everyone in the room heard what he said.

"I reckon God was pretty good to me. He favored me with the finest-looking daughters and daughter-in-law a man could hope for. I reckon I've been lucky not to have had any more trouble than I've had. I get to thinking sometimes that maybe it's not all for the best. I think a lot about maybe having trouble with such pretty girls in the house. But so far, I've been spared that misery. Darling Jill acts crazy as hell sometimes, and about nothing. But we've been living on the lucky side of the road so far."

"Now, Pa," said Griselda, "please don't start that again."

"I ain't ashamed of nothing," Ty Ty said heatedly. "I reckon Griselda is just about the prettiest girl I ever did see. There ain't a man alive who's ever seen a finer-looking pair of rising beauties as she's got. Why, man alive! They're that pretty it makes me feel sometimes like getting right down on my hands and knees like these old hound dogs you see chasing after a flowing bitch. You just ache to get down and lick something. That's the way, and it's God's own truth as He would tell it Himself if He could talk like the rest of us."

"You don't mean to sit there and say you've seen them, do you?" Will asked, winking at Griselda and Rosamond.

"Seen them? Why, man alive! I spend all my spare time trying to slip up on her when she ain't looking to see them some more. Seen them? Man alive! Just like a rabbit likes clover! And when you've seen them once, that's only the start. You can't sit calm and peaceful and think about nothing else till you see them again. And every time you see them it makes you feel just a little bit more like that old hound dog I was talking about. You're sitting out there in the yard somewhere all calm and pleased and all of a sudden you'll get a notion in your head. You sit there, telling it to go away and let you rest, and all the time there's something getting up inside of you. You can't stop it, because you can't put your hands on it; you can't talk to it, because you can't make it hear. And so it gets up and stands right there on the inside of you. Then it says something to you. It's that same old feeling again, and you know you can't stop it now to save your soul. You can sit there all day long, till it's squeezed almost to death, but it won't leave you. And that's when you go stepping around the house on your toes trying to see something. Man alive! And don't I know what I mean!"

"Aw, now, Pa," Griselda said, blushing. "You promised to stop talking like that about me."

"Girl," he said, "you just don't know how I'm praising you in my talk. I'm saying the finest things a man can say

about a woman. When a man gets that ache to get right down
on his hands and knees, and lick—well, girl, it just makes
a man—aw, shucks, Griselda."

Ty Ty fumbled in his pocket until he found a twenty-five
cent piece. He laid it in Griselda's hand.

"Take that and buy yourself a pretty the next time you're
in the city, Griselda. I wish I had more to give you."

"Now, listen here," Will said, winking at Rosamond and
Griselda. "You're giving yourself away. If you don't watch
out, you won't get a chance to see Griselda again like that.
She'll keep out of your way after this, if you don't be quiet."

"That's where you're wrong son," Ty Ty said. "I've lived
a heap longer than you have, and I know a little more about
the ways of women. Griselda won't be after keeping me from
seeing her the next time, or any time. She won't come right
out now and say so, but just the same, she'll be pleased like all
get-out when I do see her the next time. She knows good and
well I appreciate what I saw. Now, ain't that the truth, Griselda?"

"Aw, now, Pa!"

"See there? Didn't I tell you the whole truth. She'll be in
that room over there with the door wide open some of these
days before long, and I'll be standing there looking at her
for all I'm worth. A girl like her has a right to show off, too,
if she wants to. I wouldn't blame her a bit if she did. Why, man
alive! That's a sight for sore eyes!"

"Now, Pa, please stop," Griselda said, hiding her face in
her hands. "You promised to stop saying that."

Ty Ty had been so busy talking he had not noticed that
Darling Jill had got up and was pulling Dave by the hands
to the door. He jumped to his feet in an instant when he
saw the albino between him and the door. He jerked the shotgun off the chair-seat and pointed it at Dave.

"No, you don't!" he shouted. "Get back in the room where
you were, now."

"Wait a minute, Pa," Darling Jill said, running to him and
putting her arms around his neck. "Pa, just leave us alone
for a little while. He isn't going to run away. We're only going out on the back porch to get a drink and sit in the cool.
He wouldn't run away. You wouldn't run away, would you,
Dave?"

"No, you don't!" Ty Ty said, not so firmly.

"Now, Pa," Darling Jill said, hugging him tighter.

"Now, I don't know about that."

"You wouldn't run away, would you, Dave?"

The boy shook his head vigorously. He was afraid to speak to Ty Ty, but if he had dared, he would have begged to be allowed to go with Darling Jill. He continued to shake his head, hoping.

"I don't like the looks of it," Ty Ty said. "When he gets out there in the dark with nobody to guard him, all he has to do is plunge off the porch, and he's gone for good. We couldn't ever find him out there in the dark. I wouldn't like to take that risk. I don't like the looks of it."

"Let him go with her," Will said. "That's not what they're going for. He won't try to get away. He sort of likes it here now a little since Darling Jill has come home. Isn't that right, fellow?"

The boy nodded his head, trying to make them believe he was not interested in running away. He kept on nodding his head until Ty Ty laid the gun down on the chair-seat.

"I still don't like the looks of it," Ty Ty said, "but I'll have to let you go for a little while. But I'll tell you something to remember. If you do run off, it'll be hell to pay when I catch you again. I'll forge some chains around your legs and bar you in the barn so tight you'll never get another chance to leave. I aim to keep you till you locate that lode for me. You'd better not try fooling with me, because when I get mad, I stay mad."

Darling Jill drew him out of the room, pulling him by the hands. They went through the dark hall to the back porch. The water bucket was empty, and they went to the well. Dave drew the water and poured it into the bucket.

"Don't you like me better than you do your wife?" Darling Jill asked him, hanging to his arm.

"I wish I had married you," he said, his hands trembling beside her. "I didn't know there was a girl so beautiful anywhere in the country. You're the prettiest girl I've ever seen. You're so soft, and you talk like a bird-song, and you smell so good——"

They sat down on the bottom step. Shivers went over Darling Jill while she listened to Dave. She had never heard a man talk like that.

"Why are you white all over?" she asked him.

"I was born that way," he said slowly. "I can't help looking like I do."

"I think you are wonderful-looking. You don't look like any man I've ever met, and I'm glad you are so different."

"Would you marry me?" he asked huskily.

"You're already married."

"I don't want to stay that way now. I want to marry you. I like you so much and I think you are so beautiful."

"We wouldn't have to get married, if you like me a lot."

"Why?"

"Just because."

"But I couldn't do everything I wanted to."

"Don't be silly."

"I'd be a little afraid. They might beat me, or something. I don't know what they'd do to me."

"It was a shame for Pa to tie you up with ropes and bring you up here," she said. "But I'm glad he did."

"I am too, now. I wouldn't run away if I had a chance. I'm going to stay so I can see you all the time."

Darling Jill moved closer to him, putting her arm around his waist and placing her head on his shoulder. He grabbed her madly.

"Would you like to kiss me?"

"Would you let me?"

"Yes, I would like it."

He kissed her, squeezing her to him. She could feel the swell of his muscles when his body touched hers and pressed so tightly.

Presently he picked her up and started across the yard. He ran with her in the dark, not knowing where he was going.

"Where are we going?"

"Out here so they can't bother us," he said. "I don't want them to come and make me go back to the barn yet."

He walked with her to the end of the yard and sat down with her on his lap under one of the water-oak trees. She could not bear to have him release her, and she locked her arms around him.

"When we find the gold, we'll take some of it and go away together," Darling Jill said. "You would do that, wouldn't you, Dave?"

"You bet I would. I'd go now, if you'd go."

"I don't care," she whispered. "I don't care what happens. I'll do anything you ask me to."

"Why do they call you Darling Jill?" he asked after a long silence.

"When I was a little girl, everybody called me 'Darling,' and my name is Jill. When I grew up, they still called me that. Now everyone calls me Darling Jill."

"It's a perfect name for you," he said. "I couldn't think of a better name to call you. You are a darling."

"Kiss me again," she asked.

Dave bent over and drew her up until his lips touched hers. They lay on the ground unmindful of anything else in the world. The pressure of his arms and the swelling of his muscles made her tremble again and again.

Ty Ty and Will came out on the back porch looking for them. Ty Ty called, and then he swore. Will went back for a lantern, running into the house telling Ty Ty not to scare the boy away by his shouts. When he came back with the smoking lantern, Ty Ty grabbed it and started across the yard, running back and forth in all directions. He shouted to Will, swearing at Dave and Darling Jill, and looking everywhere as fast as his feet would carry him.

Rosamond and Griselda came out of the house and stood by the well looking out in the darkness.

"I knew it," Ty Ty kept saying over and over again. "I knew it all the time."

"We'll find him," Will said. "They didn't go far."

"I knew it, I just knew it. My white-haired boy is gone for fair."

"I don't believe he ran off," Will protested. "I'll bet a pretty he's only lying low till you stop scaring him to death. When they left the room, they weren't trying to run off. He was more for going out in the dark so he could have a good time with her than he was for running off. Just look for her, and you'll find him at the same time. She had her mind made up to have him, and she's the one who took him off wherever it is they've gone."

"I knew it, I just knew it was going to happen. My white-haired boy is gone for fair."

Rosamond and Griselda called from the well.

"Have you found him yet, Pa?"

Ty Ty was so busy searching for the albino he did not stop to answer.

"They're out here somewhere," Will said. "They're not far off."

Ty Ty dashed around the house, making a complete circle of it, barely missing the black mouth of the crater. He skirted the big hole by inches, almost falling into it in his blind haste.

Once around the house, he struck out across the yard, running at random. When he got out near the water-oak trees, the light from the smoking lantern suddenly revealed the snow-white hair of Dave. Ty Ty ran nearer and saw them both sprawled on the ground. Neither of them was aware of his presence, even though the yellow light flickered in Darling Jill's eyes and twinkled like two stars when her eyelids blinked.

Will saw Ty Ty standing still with the smoking lantern and he knew they had been found. He ran to see why Ty Ty was not calling him, and Rosamond and Griselda came behind.

"Did you ever see such a sight?" Ty Ty said, looking around at Will. "Now, ain't that something?"

Will waited until Griselda got there, pointing down at Dave and Darling Jill. They stood silently for a moment, trying to see in the yellow lantern light.

Ty Ty suddenly found himself turned around and being pushed towards the house.

He whirled around.

"What's the matter with you girls, Rosamond?" he said, stumbling with the lantern. "What makes you push me like that?"

"You ought to be ashamed of yourself, Pa, you and Will, standing here looking at them. Go on away, both of you, now."

Ty Ty found himself standing beside Will several yards from them.

"Now, look here," he protested; "I don't like to be shoved around like a country-cousin. What's the matter with you girls, anyhow?"

"Shame on you, Pa, you and Will," Griselda said. "You were standing here looking all the time. Now, go on off and stop looking."

"Well, I'll be a suck-egg mule," Ty Ty said. "I wasn't doing a thing in the world but standing there. And here you girls come running up and say, 'Shame on me.' I ain't done a blessed thing to be ashamed of. What's wrong with you Griselda and Rosamond?"

Will and Ty Ty moved away, walking slowly towards the house. Just before reaching the well, Ty Ty stopped and looked back.

"Now, what in God's name did I do wrong?"

"Women don't like men to stand around and see one of them getting it," Will said. "That's why they raised such a howl about you being there. They only wanted to get me and you away."

"Well, dog my cats," Ty Ty said. "Is that what was going on back there! I never would have known it, Will, I declare

I wouldn't. I only thought they was lying there hugging one another. That's the truth if I know it. I couldn't see a thing in that pale light."

Chapter X

THEY HAD BEEN AT WORK since sunrise in the new crater, and at eleven o'clock the heat was blistering. Buck and Shaw had little to say to Will. They had never been able to get along together, and even the prospect of turning up a shovelful of yellow nuggets any moment did not serve to bind them any closer. If Buck had had his way, Will would never have been sent for in the first place. All the gold that was turned up was going into their own pockets, anyway; if Will should try to take some, they would die fighting before they would allow him to share in it.

Will leaned on his shovel and watched Shaw pick the clay. He laughed a little, but neither Buck nor Shaw paid the least attention to him. They went on as though he were nowhere near.

"It looks to me like you boys would have better sense than to let Ty Ty egg you on to digging all these big holes in the ground. He gets all this hard work out of you, and it doesn't cost him a penny. Why don't you boys go off somewhere and get a real job that pays something when Saturday comes? You don't want to stay countrymen all your lives, do you? Tell Ty Ty to shovel his own dirt, and walk off."

"Go to hell, you lint-head," Shaw said.

Will rolled a cigarette while he watched them dig and sweat. He did not mind being called a lint-head by people in his own world, but he could never stand being called that by Buck and Shaw. They knew it was the quickest and most effective way either to silence him outright or to make him fighting mad.

Buck looked up at the rim of the crater to see if Ty Ty were near. If there was going to be trouble, he wished to have Ty Ty there to help him. Their father had always sided with them when they had an argument with Will, and he would this time as well.

But Ty Ty was not within sight. He was over in the new-ground with the two colored men trying to get the cotton banked. The crop had been planted late that year, as they had been so busy digging that there had been no opportunity to plant it until June, and Ty Ty wished to hurry it along as much as possible, if it was within his power to make it grow and mature, in order to get some money by the first of September. He had already bought to the limit of his credit in the stores at Marion, and he had been unable to get a loan at the bank. If the cotton did not thrive, or if the boll weevils ruined it, he did not know what he was going to do the coming fall and winter. There were two mules to feed, in addition to the two colored families, and his own household.

"There ain't no more gold in this ground than there is in the toes of my socks," Will said derisively. "Why don't you boys go up to Augusta or Atlanta or somewhere and have a good time? I'll be damned if I'd stay a clodhopper all my life just because Ty Ty Walden wants you to dig in the ground for him."

"Aw, go to hell, you Valley town lint-head."

Will looked at Buck, debating momentarily whether to hit him.

"Got any message to send your folks?" he asked finally.

"If you want to play the dozens, you're at the right homestead," Shaw said.

Will threw down his shovel with both hands and picked up a dried clod of clay. He ran several steps toward them, rolling the dead cigarette to the corner of his mouth with his tongue.

"I didn't come over here to have trouble with you boys, but if you're looking for it, you're barking up the right tree now."

"That's all you've ever done," Shaw said, gripping the shovel handle in both hands. "Barking is all you've ever done."

Will wished to fight Buck, if there was going to be a fight. He had nothing against Shaw, but Shaw would side with his brother always. Will disliked Buck. He had disliked him from the first. He did not hate him personally, but Griselda was Buck's wife, and Buck was always standing between them. They had already had several tussles, not over Griselda any more than for any other reason, and they were likely to have others. As long as Griselda was married to Buck, and lived with him, Will would fight him whenever he had the opportunity.

"Drop that clod," Buck ordered.

"Come and make me," Will retorted.

Buck stepped back and whispered something to Shaw. Will

stepped forward and threw the clod with all his might just as Buck ran towards him with the raised shovel. The shovel handle struck Will a glancing blow on the shoulder, flying off to the ground. The clod had missed Buck, but it hit Shaw squarely in the pit of the stomach. He bent over with pain, falling to the ground and groaning weakly.

When Buck turned and saw Shaw doubled into a knot behind him, he thought surely Will had injured him seriously. He ran forward, raising the shovel over his head, and hit Will on the forehead with all his might.

The blow stunned Will, but it did not knock him out. He was up on his feet, angrier than ever, and running after Buck before the shovel could be raised for another blow.

"All you damn Waldens think you're tough, but we're tougher where I come from," Will said. "It would take you and six more like you to beat me up. I'm used to it—I have a couple of fights every morning before breakfast where I come from."

"You damn lint-head," Buck said contemptuously.

Shaw got to his hands and knees, blinking his eyes. He looked around for a weapon of any nature, but there was nothing within his reach. His shovel was on the other side of Will.

"You damn lint-head," Buck repeated, sneering.

"Come on, both of you sons-of-bitches," Will shouted. "I'll take you both down at the same time. I wasn't raised to be scared of countrymen."

Buck raised his shovel, but Will reached up and jerked it out of his hands, tossing it out of reach behind him. With a well-aimed blow he struck Buck on the jaw, knocking him flat on his back. Shaw ran towards him, crouched low over his knees. Will swung at him with both fists, one after the other. Shaw's knees gave way, and he fell at Will's feet.

Buck was up again. He jumped on Will, hurling him to the ground and pinning his arms under him. Before Will could twist free, Buck had begun pounding him on the head and back. All of them were in an ugly temper by that time.

From the top of the crater Ty Ty shouted at them. He came running down the side at once, jumping into the midst of the fists and kicks. He pried Buck and Will apart, and flung them sprawling to the ground on each side of him. Ty Ty was as large as any one of the others, and he had always been able to handle a fight between them. He stood panting and blowing, looking down at them.

"That's enough of that," he said, still breathing hard.

"What in the pluperfect hell have you boys got to fight about so much, anyhow? That ain't digging for the lode. Fighting among yourselves won't find it."

Buck sat up and held his swollen jaw. He glared at Will, still undefeated.

"Send him back where he belongs, then," Buck said. "The son-of-a-bitch hasn't any business over here. This ain't no place for lint-heads to hang out."

"I'll go when I get damn good and ready and not a minute before. Just try and make me go before then. Just try it!"

"What in the pluperfect hell did you boys go and do that for, anyhow?" Ty Ty asked Shaw, turning to see if he was all right. "There ain't nothing for you boys to fight about like this. When we strike the lode, it's all going to be divided up fair and square, and nobody is going to get a larger share than the next one. I aim to see to that. Now, what made you boys start scrapping one another like that?"

"Nothing started it, Pa," Shaw said. "And it wasn't about sharing the gold. It wasn't about anything like that. It just happened, that's all. Every time that son-of-a-bitch comes over here he invites a beating. It's just the way he talks and acts. He acts like he's better than we are, or something. He acts like he's better because he works in a cotton mill. He's always calling Buck and me countrymen."

"Now that ain't nothing to get all heated up about," Ty Ty said. "Boys, it's a shame we can't keep a peaceful family all the time. That's what I've aimed all my life to have."

"Make him leave Griselda alone then," Buck said.

"Is Griselda in this?" Ty Ty asked in wonder. "Why, I didn't know she was all mixed up in this fight."

"You're a damn liar," Will shouted. "I never said a word about her."

"Now, boys," Ty Ty said, "don't start scrapping all over again. What's Griselda got to do with all this?"

"Well, he didn't say anything about her," Buck replied, "but it's just the way he looks and acts. He acts like he's getting ready to do something to her."

"That's a lie," Will shouted.

"Now, Buck, you maybe just imagine all that. I know it ain't so, because Will is married to Rosamond and they get along first-rate together. He ain't after Griselda. Just forget that part."

Will looked at Buck but said nothing. He was angry because Ty Ty had separated them before he could strike the last blow.

"If he would stay where he belongs, and not come over here raising hell, I'd be satisfied," Buck stated. "The son-of-a-bitch is a lint-head, anyway. He ought to stay with his own kind. We don't want to mix with him."

Will got to his feet again, looking around for the shovel.

Ty Ty ran and pushed him to the other side of the crater. He held Will with both hands, pushing him back against the side of the hole.

"Will," he said calmly, "don't pay any attention to Buck. That heat's got his dander up, and about nothing. Now stay here and leave him alone."

He ran back to the other side of the hole and pushed Buck down. Shaw was out of it then. He made no further signs of going in again.

"You boys all get up on top of the ground and cool off," Ty Ty ordered. "You got all heated up down here in the hole, and fresh air is the only way to get it out of you. Now go on up there and cool off a while."

He waited while Buck and Shaw climbed out and disappeared from sight. After giving them plenty of time to get away, he urged Will to get up and climb to the top for air. Ty Ty followed close behind in case Shaw and Buck were waiting just out of sight to jump on Will and resume the fight. When they got to the surface above, Shaw and Buck had gone from sight.

"Don't give them no more thought, Will," he said. "Just sit down in the shade and cool off."

They went to the side of the house and sat down in the shade. Will was still angry, but he was willing to drop the fight where it was, even if Buck had had the last blow. The sooner he got back to Scottsville the better would he be pleased. He would never have come in the first place if Rosamond and Darling Jill had not begged him so much. Now he wished to get back to the Valley and talk to his friends before the meeting of the local Friday night. The sight of bare land, cultivated and fallow, with never a factory or mill to be seen, made him a little sick in the stomach.

"You ain't made up your mind to leave so soon, have you, Will?" Ty Ty asked. "I hope you ain't aiming to do that."

"Sure, I'm leaving," Will said. "I can't be wasting my time digging holes in the ground. I'm no damn doodlebug."

"I aimed to have you help us till we struck the lode, Will. I need all the help I can get right now. The lode is there, sure as God made little green apples, and I ache to get my hands on it. I've been waiting fifteen years, night and day, for just that."

"You ought to be out making cotton," Will said shortly. "You can raise more cotton on this land in a year than you can find gold in a lifetime. It's a waste of everything to dig these holes all over the place."

"I wish now I had spent a little more time on the cotton. It looks like now that I'm going to be short of money before the lode is struck. If I had twenty or thirty bales of cotton to tide me over the fall and winter, I could devote all the rest of the time to digging. I sure do need a lot of cotton to sell the first of September."

"Well, it's too late to plant any more cotton this year. You're out of luck, if you don't do something else."

"There ain't but one thing I can do, and that's dig."

"This house is going to topple over into the hole if you dig much more in it. The house is leaning a little now. It won't take much to tip it over."

Ty Ty looked at the pine logs that had been dragged from the woods and propped against the building. The logs were large enough and strong enough to hold the house where it was, but if it were undermined too much, it would surely fall in, and then turn over. When it did that, it would either be lying on one side in the big hole, or else it would be upside down on the bottom of it.

"Will, when the gold-fever strikes a man, he can't think about nothing else to save his soul. I reckon that's what's wrong with me, if anything is. I've got the fever so bad I can't be bothered about planting cotton. I'm bent on getting those little yellow nuggets out of the ground. Come heaven, hell, or high water, I reckon I'll just have to keep on digging till I strike the lode. I can't stop to do nothing else now. The gold-fever has water-logged me through and through."

Will had cooled off. He was no longer restless to get up, and he did not care whether he ever saw Buck and Shaw again to renew the fight. He was willing to let them alone until the next time.

"If you're hard up for money, why don't you go up to Augusta and borrow some from Jim Leslie?"

"Do what, Will?" Ty Ty asked.

"Get Jim Leslie to lend you enough to see you through the fall and winter. You can plant a big crop of cotton next spring."

"Aw, shucks, Will," Ty Ty said, laughing a little, "there wouldn't be no sense in that."

"Why not? He's got plenty of money, and his wife is as rich as a manure pile."

"He wouldn't help me none, Will."

"How do you know he wouldn't? You've never tried to borrow off of him, have you? Well, how do you know he wouldn't lend you a little?"

"Jim Leslie won't speak to me on the street, Will," he replied sadly, "and if he won't speak to me on the street, I know durn well he wouldn't lend me money. Wouldn't be no sense in trying to ask him. It would be just a big waste of time trying."

"Hell, he's your boy, ain't he? Well, if he's your boy, he ought to listen to you when you tell him how much hard luck you're having trying to strike the lode."

"That wouldn't make much difference to Jim Leslie now. He left home just on that account. He said he wasn't going to stay here and be made a fool of digging for nuggets all his life. I don't reckon he's changed much since then, either."

"How long ago was that?"

"Nearly fifteen years ago, I reckon."

"All that's worn off of him by this time. He'll be tickled to death to see you. You're his daddy, ain't you?"

"Yes, I reckon. But that won't make much difference to him. I've tried to speak to him on the street, but he won't look my way at all."

"I'll bet he'll listen to you when you tell him about the hard luck, anyway."

"Well, this here now lode might turn up, if I could afford to keep digging," Ty Ty said, rising to his feet.

"Sure, it might," Will told him. "That's just what I've been trying to make you see."

"If I had a little money, maybe two or three hundred dollars, this here now lode might could be located. It takes time, and a durn heap of patience to locate gold, Will."

"Why don't you go up to Augusta and talk to him about it then? That's the thing to do."

Ty Ty started around the house. He stopped at the corner and waited for Will to catch up with him. They went across the yard and down to the barn where Dave and Uncle Felix were. Shaw and Buck were sitting on the stall partition talking to the albino and Uncle Felix.

"Boys," Ty Ty said, "we've got to be up and doing. I've made up my mind to go up to Augusta right away. Come and wash up some so we can get started."

"What for?" Buck asked sourly.

"What for? Why, to see Jim Leslie, son."

"I reckon I'll stay here then," Buck stated.

"Now, boys," Ty Ty pleaded, "I need you to drive me up there in the car. You know good and well I can't drive an automobile in the big city. Why, I'd wreck the whole shooting-match up there the first thing off the bat."

First Buck and then Shaw climbed down off the stall partition and left the barn. Ty Ty walked behind them, telling them over and over his reason for wishing to see Jim Leslie.

Will stuck his head through the feed-rack and looked at Dave.

"How you feeling, fellow?"

"All right," the boy said.

"Would you like to get out and go home now?"

"I'd rather stay here."

Will pulled his head out, laughing at the albino. He turned away, walking out the barn towards the house.

"You might just as well cool your heels a while," he called back. "Darling Jill won't be here tonight. She's going up to Augusta with the rest of us."

He left Dave and Uncle Felix with no other word. On the way to the house he began to feel sorry for Dave. He hoped Ty Ty would turn him free in a few days and let him go back home if he wished to.

Buck was on the back porch washing his face and hands in the basin, but Will did not look in that direction. He went around to the front of the house and sat down on the steps to wait for Ty Ty to get ready to leave. Pluto had gone home that morning to change his shirt and socks, and Will missed him. He said something about getting an early start to canvass for votes, and Will hoped he would come by the house before they left. Pluto might be elected sheriff, if his friends who expected to be appointed deputies worked hard enough for him. But Pluto alone could never gather enough support.

Griselda was the first to come out of the house ready to leave. She smiled at Will, and he winked at her. She was wearing a new floral print afternoon frock with a large hat that had a brim covering her shoulders. Will wondered if he had ever seen a girl so good-looking as Griselda. He hated to think of having to go back to Scottsville without having an opportunity of seeing her alone. He might even have to come back with them that night from Augusta, instead of going to the Valley, just so he could have the chance of being with her.

Chapter XI

WHEN THEY REACHED Augusta in the early evening, Buck stopped the car at the curb on Broad Street near Sixth. Nothing had been said about stopping downtown, and Ty Ty leaned forward to ask Buck and Shaw why they had stopped. Jim Leslie's house was on The Hill, several miles away.

"What did you do this for, Buck?"

"I'm getting out here to go to the movies," Buck answered, not looking around. "I'm not going up there to Jim Leslie's."

Shaw got out with him and they stood on the street. They waited to see if anyone else was going with them. After a moment's hesitation, Darling Jill and Rosamond got out.

"Now, you folks wait a minute," Ty Ty said excitedly. "You folks are just going to shove it all off on me. Why can't somebody go with me up there and help convince Jim Leslie how much in need of money I am?"

"I'll go with you, Pa," Griselda said.

"You won't need me," Will stated, getting out. "I couldn't talk to him without getting mad and batting him down."

"Go on with Pa, Will," Darling Jill urged. "Pa needs you along."

"Why don't you go? You're telling everybody else to go, but you don't go yourself."

"Don't be scared of Jim Leslie, Will," Griselda said. "He can't hurt you."

"Who said I was scared of anybody? Me—scared of him?"

"It's time to go," Ty Ty said. "We'll be sitting here arguing all night if we don't make up our minds right away."

Buck and Shaw started up the street towards the brightly lighted theaters. Rosamond ran and caught up with them.

"Oh, I'll go," Darling Jill said. "I don't mind."

"We three are enough, unless Will wants to go."

"That's all right with me," Will said. "I'll hang around here till you get back."

Darling Jill got out of the back seat and sat under the steeringwheel. Griselda got in with her, leaving Ty Ty alone in the rear.

"I'll stick around here somewhere," Will said, looking up and down the street.

He walked slowly away, keeping close to the curb and glancing up at the windows on the second storeys. The buildings all had iron-grilled balconies, three or four feet wide, and people were sitting in the windows and leaning over the iron railings looking down on the sidewalk.

Somebody further down the street called Will's name. He walked down there, looking up at the faces overhead.

"There goes Will," Griselda said hopelessly.

One of the girls overhead was leaning over the railing talking to him. Will walked away looking up at other balconies. The girl who had tried to talk to him cursed and called him all the obscene names she could think of.

Darling Jill giggled and whispered something to Griselda. They spoke in undertones for a while, and Ty Ty was unable to overhear a word they said.

"Let's be going, girls," he said. "It's a sin and a shame to stay here."

Darling Jill made no effort to start the car. One of the girls above them on the balcony was pointing at Ty Ty. He had already seen them up there, and he refused to look in any direction except down at his feet.

He was biting his tongue with fear that one of the girls up there would speak to him before Darling Jill would start the car.

"Hello, grandpa," the girl who had pointed said. "Come on up a while and have a good time."

Ty Ty looked at Darling Jill and Griselda when they turned to see what he was going to do. He was wishing they would only hurry and drive away before the girls on the second-storey balconies could say anything else to him. He would not have minded being spoken to under any other circumstance, but he did not feel free to answer anybody up there while he was with Darling Jill and Griselda. He leaned forward, poking Darling Jill with his finger, urging her to drive away.

"Why don't you go up there and see what's going on, Pa?" she asked, giggling again.

"Man alive!" Ty Ty said, blushing through his tanned skin.

"Go on up, Pa," Griselda urged. "We'll wait for you. Go on up and have a good time."

"Man alive!" Ty Ty said again. "I'm 'way past that age. Wouldn't be no sense in that."

The girl who had been watching Ty Ty beckoned to him

with her finger, jerking her head and pointing to the stairs that opened on the street. She was a small girl, not much older than sixteen or seventeen, and when she leaned over the iron railing and looked down into the car, Ty Ty could not keep from glancing up and wishing he could go up the stairs to see her. His hands clutched the thin roll of soiled one-dollar bills in his pocket, and perspiration dampened his brow. He knew Darling Jill and Griselda were waiting for him to get out and walk up the stairs, but he did not have the courage to go in their presence.

"Don't be a tightwad, grandpa," the girl said out of the corner of her lips. "You'll never be young but once."

Ty Ty glanced at the backs of Griselda's and Darling Jill's heads. They were watching the girl on the balcony above, and talking about her in undertones.

"Go on up, Pa," Griselda said. "You'll have a good time up there. You ought to have a little fun sometimes after working so hard at home in the holes."

"Now, Griselda," Ty Ty protested weakly, "I'm 'way past that now. Don't tease me so much. It makes me feel like I don't know what I'm liable to do with myself."

The girl had left the little iron-grilled balcony. Ty Ty looked up and felt a relief. He leaned forward, prodding Darling Jill with his finger, urging her to drive away.

"Wait just another minute," she said.

He could see that they were watching the stairs that opened on the street. Out of the gray darkness of the building the girl suddenly appeared in the glow of the whiteway lights.

Ty Ty saw her and sank down in the seat hoping to get out of sight. She walked straight for the automobile, stepping off the curb and into the street beside Ty Ty on the back seat.

"I know what's wrong with you—you're bashful."

Ty Ty blushed and sank lower. He could see Darling Jill and Griselda watching him in the little mirror on top of the windshield.

"Come on upstairs and jazz a little."

Darling Jill giggled outright.

Ty Ty said something, but no one could hear what it was. The girl put her foot on the runningboard and reached for Ty Ty's arm to pull him out. He moved to the middle of the seat, evading her fingers.

Darling Jill turned around and glanced at the girl's powdered breasts in the low-cut dress. She turned back and whispered something to Griselda. Both laughed.

"What's the matter with you, grandpa? Have you got a boil on you, or don't you have any money?"

Ty Ty vaguely wondered if she would go away and let him alone if he told her he had no money.

He shook his head at her, moving further away.

"You're a cheap son-of-a-bitch," she said. "Why can't you spend a little money at the end of the week? If I had known you were such a tight-fisted son-of-a-bitch I wouldn't have bothered to come down here."

Ty Ty did not answer her, and he thought she would go on back into the building. She did not even remove her foot from the runningboard, but stood waiting beside the car and looking sullenly at him.

"Let's go, girls," he urged. "We've got to be on our way."

Darling Jill started the motor and engaged the gears. She turned around to see if the girl had removed her foot from the car. She backed several feet. The girl's foot was dragged off the runningboard, and she stood at the curb cursing Ty Ty. When they were clear of the curbing, Darling Jill started down the street and turned the corner. In a few minutes they were in a boulevard bound for The Hill.

"I'm sure thankful you girls got me away from there," Ty Ty said. "It looked like we was never going to get away. I'd have gone up there with her just to make her be quiet if we hadn't left when we did. I hate to be out in the main street and have a woman swear at me like that for all the people to hear. I never could stand being cussed by a woman right in the middle of the city."

"Oh, we weren't going to let you go up there, Pa," Griselda said. "We were only fooling. We wouldn't have let you go up there and get diseased. It was only a joke on you."

"Well, I ain't saying I wanted to go, and I ain't saying I didn't. But I sure hate to have a woman swear at me like that on the main street. It doesn't sound nice, for one thing. I never could put up with it."

They crossed the canal and entered another boulevard. The Hill was still two miles distant, but the car was in a fast-moving stream of traffic, and they sped up the gradually rising elevation. Ty Ty was still a little nervous after his encounter with the girl who lived in the room behind the iron balcony, and he was glad it was over. He had known several girls who lived in that part of town, but that was ten to fifteen years earlier, and the ones he knew had gone away and others much younger had taken their places. Ty Ty felt uneasy in the presence of the new generation of girls down there, because they were no longer willing to stay in their rooms, or even on the balconies. Now they came down to the street and dragged men out of their cars. He shook his head, glad he was in another section of the city.

"Man alive!" Ty Ty said. "She was a she-devil, all right. I don't know when I've seen such a regular little hell-cat."

"Are you still thinking about that girl, Pa?" Griselda asked. "If you say so, we'll turn around and go back."

"Great guns," he shouted, "don't do that! Keep on the way we're going. I've got to see Jim Leslie. I can't be fooling away my time down there again."

"Do you know which way to go now?" Darling Jill asked him, slowing down at an intersection of three streets.

"Take the right-hand one," he said, pointing with his hand.

They drove for several blocks along a tree-lined street. There were large houses in that part of the city. Some of the large houses occupied an entire block. Up above them they could see the high towers on the Bon Air-Vanderbilt. They were in the midst of the resort hotels.

"It's a big white house with three storeys and a big front porch," Ty Ty said. "Now go slow while I look out for it."

They drove two more blocks in silence.

"They all look alike at night," Ty Ty said. "But when I see Jim Leslie's, I'll know it without fail."

Darling Jill slowed down to cross a street. Just beyond was a large white house with three storeys and a large porch with white columns rising to the roof.

"That's it," Ty Ty said, prodding them with his finger. "That's Jim Leslie's as sure as God makes little green apples. Stop right where we are."

They got out and looked up at the big white house behind the trees. There were lights in all the windows downstairs, and in some of the windows on the middle floor. The front door was open, but the screen door was closed. Ty Ty became worried about the screen door. He was afraid it was locked.

"Don't stop to knock or ring a bell, girls. If we did that, Jim Leslie might see who we are and lock the door before we can get inside."

Ty Ty went ahead and tiptoed up the steps and across the wide porch. Darling Jill and Griselda stayed close behind so they would not be locked outside. Ty Ty opened the screen door noiselessly, and they went into the wide hall.

"We're on the inside," Ty Ty whispered, much relieved.

"He'll have a hard time putting us out now before I can tell him what I'm after."

They walked slowly to the wide door on the right. Ty Ty stopped there, looking into the room.

Jim Leslie heard them and glanced up from the book he was reading with a frown on his face. He was alone in the room at the time. His wife was somewhere else in the house, probably on the floor above, Ty Ty supposed.

He walked into the room with his son.

"What are you doing here?" Jim Leslie said. "You know I don't let you come here. Get out!"

He glanced over Ty Ty's shoulder and saw his sister and Griselda. He frowned again, looking at them harder still.

"Now, Jim Leslie," Ty Ty began, "you know you're pleased to see us. We ain't seen you in a long long time, now have we, son?"

"Who let you in?"

"We let ourselves in. The door was open, and I knew you were here, because I saw you through the window, so we just walked in. That's the way we do out at home. Nobody ever has to knock on my door, or ring bells either, to come into the house. Out there everybody is welcome."

Jim Leslie looked again at Griselda. He had seen her once or twice before, at a distance, but he had not realized that she was so pretty. He wondered why a girl so beautiful had married Buck and had gone to live in the country. She would have looked much more at home in a house like this. He sat down, and the others found seats for themselves.

"What did you come here for?" he asked his father.

"It's important, son," Ty Ty said. "You know good and well I wouldn't come to your house uninvited unless I was in great trouble."

"Money, I suppose," Jim Leslie said. "Why don't you dig it out of the ground?"

"It's in there, all right, but I just can't seem to get it out right away."

"That's what you thought ten or twelve years ago. It looks like you ought to learn some sense in fifteen years. There's no gold out there. I told you that before I left."

"Gold or no gold, I've got the fever, son, and I can't stop digging. But you're wrong about that, because the gold is there, if I could only locate it. I've got an albino now, though, and I'm aiming to strike the lode any day now. All the folks say an albino can divine it if it's in the country."

Jim Leslie grunted disgustedly. He looked helplessly at his father, not knowing what to say to a man who talked so foolishly.

"Don't be a damn fool all your life," he said finally. "That talk about diviners is Negroes' talk. They're the only people I ever heard of who took such things seriously. A white man ought to have better sense than to fall for such superstition. You grow worse every year."

"You might call it that, but I'm going about the digging of the nuggets scientifically. I've done that clear from the start. The way I'm doing is scientific, and I know it is."

Jim Leslie had nothing further to say about it. He turned and looked at the bookcase.

Ty Ty looked around at the richly furnished room. He had never been in the house before, and its rugs and furnishings were a revelation to him. The rugs were as soft and yielding as freshly plowed ground, and he walked over them feeling at home. He turned once to look at Griselda and Darling Jill, but they were watching Jim Leslie and did not meet his eyes.

Presently Jim Leslie slumped down in the large overstuffed chair. He locked his hands under his chin and studied Griselda. Ty Ty saw that he was looking at her steadily.

Chapter XII

"THAT'S BUCK'S WIFE, GRISELDA," Ty Ty said.

"I know," Jim Leslie replied without turning.

"She's a mighty pretty girl."

"I know."

"The first time I saw her I said to myself: 'Man alive! Griselda is a mighty pleasing dish to set before a man.'"

"I know," he said again.

"It's a shame your wife ain't so pretty as Griselda," Ty Ty said sympathetically. "It's a dog-gone shame, Jim Leslie, if I do say it myself."

Jim Leslie shrugged his shoulders a little, still looking at Griselda. He could not keep his eyes away from her.

"They tell me that your wife has got diseased," Ty Ty said, moving his chair closer to his son's. "I've heard the boys say a lot of these rich people up here on The Hill have got one thing and another wrong with them. It's a dog-gone shame you had to marry her, Jim Leslie. I feel downright sorry for you, son. Did she get you cornered so you couldn't worm out of marrying her?"

"I don't know," Jim Leslie said wearily.

"I sure hate to see you married to a diseased wife, son. Now just look at those two girls, there. Neither of them is diseased. Darling Jill is all right, and so is Griselda. And Rosamond ain't diseased either. They're all nice clean girls, son, the three of them. I'd hate to have a girl in my house diseased. I'd feel so ashamed of it that I'd hide my face when people came to see me at the house. It must be pretty hard for you to have to live with a diseased woman like your wife. Why is it, anyhow, that so many of these rich girls here in Augusta have got the diseases, son?"

"I don't know," he replied weakly.

"What is it she's got, anyhow?"

Jim Leslie tried to laugh at Ty Ty, but he could not even force a smile to his lips.

"Don't you know the name of it, son?"

Jim Leslie shook his head, indicating that he had no answer to give.

"The boys said she has gonorrhea. Is that right, son? That's what I heard, if I remember right."

Jim Leslie nodded his head almost imperceptibly. As long as he could sit there and look at Griselda he was willing to let Ty Ty's questions pass over his head. He had no interest in them as long as Griselda was there.

"Well, I'm sorry for you, son. It's a dog-gone shame you had to marry a girl with a disease. I reckon, though, you wouldn't have done it if she hadn't cornered you so you couldn't worm out of it. If you couldn't get out of it, then that's something God Himself couldn't have helped. You deserve a little better, though. It's a dog-gone shame you had to do it."

Ty Ty moved his chair closer to Jim Leslie's. He leaned forward, nodding his head towards Griselda.

"It's a dog-gone shame about your wife, son, if I do say it myself. Now, just take Griselda, there. She ain't diseased, and she's the prettiest girl you can ever hope to see. Just look at her! Now, you know good and well you've never seen a prettier girl, all over, have you, son?"

Jim Leslie smiled, but said nothing.

"Aw, now, Pa," Griselda begged anxiously, "please don't

say those things again now. Don't say things like that in front of him, Pa. It's not nice, Pa."

"Now you just wait, Griselda. I'm mighty proud of you, and I aim to praise you. We ain't strangers here, anyhow. Ain't Jim Leslie one of the family, just like Darling Jill, there, and the rest of them? I aim to praise you mightily, Griselda. I'm as proud of you as a hen is of a lone chick."

"But don't say any more then, please, Pa."

"Son," Ty Ty said, turning towards Jim Leslie, "Griselda is the prettiest girl in the whole State of Georgia, and I reckon that's something to be proud of. Why, man alive! She's got the finest pair of rising beauties a man ever laid eyes on. If you could see them there under the cloth, you'd know I'm telling the truth as only God Himself could tell it if He could only talk. And you wouldn't be the first one to go plumb wild just looking at them, either."

"Oh, Pa!" Griselda begged, covering her face and trying to hide from sight. "Please don't say any more, Pa. Please don't!"

"Now you just sit and be quiet while I praise you mightily, Griselda. I know what I'm doing. I'm proud to discuss you, too. Jim Leslie has never seen the likes of what I'm talking about. His wife don't appear to be in the running at all. She looks like she's all mashed down on the chest and can't rise up. It's a shame and a pity, I'll be dog-gone if it ain't, that he had to marry a girl with her awful looks. It's a wonder he can stand it, on top of the disease. Now, don't try to stop me while I'm praising you, Griselda. I'm mighty proud of you, and I aim to praise you sky-high."

Griselda was already beginning to cry a little. Her shoulders shook in jerks and she had to hold the handkerchief tight against her eyes so the tears would not fall on her lap,

"Son," Ty Ty said, "ain't she the prettiest little girl you ever did see? When I was a young man, I used to think that all girls were alike, more or less, after allowing for a little natural difference, and I reckon maybe you've thought the same up till now; but when you've got an eyeful of Griselda, there, you know durn well you've been missing a heap thinking such foolishness all your life. Son, I reckon you know what I mean. You sit there and look at her and you get to feeling something trying to stand up on the inside of you. That's it. I ain't been around much outside of Georgia, and so I can't speak for the other parts of the world, but I've sure-God seen a heap in my time in Georgia and I'm here to tell you that it ain't no use to go no further away when it comes to looking for such prettiness. Man alive! Griselda totes around with her so much prettiness that it's a shame to look sometimes."

Griselda cried brokenly.

Ty Ty felt in his pocket for a quarter, finally picking it out of a handful of nails, harness brads, and loose change. He gave it to Griselda.

"Now, ain't I right, Jim Leslie?"

Jim Leslie glanced at his father and back again at Griselda. He appeared to be far less angry with his father than he had been earlier in the evening. He wished he could say something to Griselda, or to Ty Ty about her.

"Maybe that wasn't a fair question," Ty Ty said. "I reckon I'd best take that back, son. You ain't had a chance to see Griselda like I have, and you can't be expected to take my word for what you ain't seen. When the time comes to see her, though, you'll remember that I didn't lie about it, not one word. She's got all the prettiness I said she has, and then some. If you'll just sit there and look at her, you'll get to feeling it in no time. Her prettiness comes right through everything if you're there to see it."

Jim Leslie suddenly sat up and listened. There was the distinct sound of a person walking somewhere in the house. He jumped to his feet, nodding almost imperceptibly at Darling Jill and Griselda, and ran from the room.

Darling Jill got up and walked across the room and stood by the mantelpiece looking at the bric-a-brac. She turned and called Griselda.

"Did you ever see such beautiful things in all your life, Griselda?"

"But we shouldn't touch anything, Darling Jill. None of it is ours. It belongs to them."

"Jim Leslie is my brother, so why shouldn't we do what we like in his house?"

"It's her house, too."

Darling Jill turned up her nose and made a face that both Griselda and Ty Ty could plainly see.

"Jim Leslie lives in fine style all right," Ty Ty said. "Just look at all the fine furniture in this room. To look at him now, a man wouldn't think that he came from out near Marion when he was a boy. I don't reckon he's got all the way used to such things, though. I'll bet a pretty he wishes sometimes he was out at home with Buck and Shaw and the rest of us helping dig in the holes. Jim Leslie ain't no different from the whole of us, Griselda. Don't let a fine suit of clothes try to tell you different. I wouldn't be scared in his house if I was you."

Darling Jill put her hand on the mahogany end-table and felt the smooth beauty of it. She called Griselda to admire it with her.

"There is a picture as big as a window sash," Ty Ty remarked, getting up and going to the wall to inspect it more closely. "Now, it took a lot of time and patience to do a job like that. I'll bet there was two months' work put into that. Just look at all the trees with red leaves."

They looked for a moment at the landscape Ty Ty admired so much, and went to the windows to look at the curtains. Ty Ty was left to himself, puzzled over the oil painting. He stood back and looked at it with his head to one side, and then he walked closer to study the texture of it. He liked the picture best of anything he had noticed in the house.

"The man who painted that knew what he was doing, all right," Ty Ty said. "He didn't put in all the limbs on the trees, but I'll be dog-goned if he didn't make the picture more like a real woods than woods really are. I've never seen a grove of trees like that in all my life, but dog-gone if it ain't better than the real thing. I sure would like to have a picture like that out at Marion. Those old Black-Draught calendars ain't nothing once you have seen a picture like this. Even those Coca-Cola signs they put up around Marion look pretty sick up beside something fine like this. I sure wish I could persuade Jim Leslie to part with it and let me take it home with me tonight."

"Pa, please don't ask for anything," Griselda begged in haste. "All this belongs to her, too."

"If Jim Leslie wants to give me something out of the bounty of his heart, I'll take it. And if she tries to stop me, then I'll just be compelled to ride right over her. What do I care for her!"

Ty Ty turned about, and in turning he knocked a china vase from a little table he had not known was in existence. He looked quickly at Darling Jill and Griselda.

"Now I've gone and done it," he said meekly. "What will Jim Leslie say to that!"

"Quick," Griselda said, "we must pick up every piece before she comes into the room."

She and Ty Ty got down on the floor and swept the chips of thin china into a pile. Darling Jill would not help. She acted as though she did not care whether the pieces were picked up or left lying on the floor for everyone to see. Ty Ty trembled all over when he thought of what Jim Leslie's wife would say if she saw what he had so carelessly done.

"Where in the world can we put the pieces?" Griselda asked excitedly.

Ty Ty looked wildly around the room. He did not know what he was looking for, but the windows were closed and he saw the fireplace held no ashes to bury them in.

"Here," he said, holding out both hands. "Put everything in here."

"But what are we going to do with them?"

Ty Ty slipped the broken china into his pocket, smiling up at both of them. He walked away holding the pocket with his hand.

"That's the finest place in the world. When we get on the outside of town, I'll just cast them away and won't nobody ever know the difference."

Darling Jill looked into the next room through the wide glass doors. She could see nothing in the darkness, but she imagined it was the dining-room. Both she and Griselda wished to see everything they could during the short time they would be there.

Ty Ty sat down in a chair to wait for Jim Leslie's return. He had been gone for ten or fifteen minutes, and Ty Ty was anxious for him to come back. He felt lost in the big house.

Jim Leslie came to the door. Ty Ty got up and walked toward his son.

"What did you wish to see me about?"

"Well, I'm hard up, son. Black Sam and Uncle Felix didn't get much cotton planted this year, what with taking time off every day or so to dig some for the lode on their own account, and when September comes, I won't hardly have a red penny to my name. I'm aiming to strike that lode out there any day now, but I can't say when it will be. And I need a little money to tide me over."

"I can't be lending you money, Pa. All I've got is tied up in real estate, and it takes all I can make from day to day to run this house. You've got the impression that people here in Augusta go around carrying big rolls of money with them, and that's wrong; people with money have to invest it, and when it's invested, you just can't pick it up one moment and lay it down the next."

"Your wife has got some."

"Well, I suppose she has, but it's not mine."

Jim Leslie turned and looked down the hall as though he expected to see Gussie. She was still in another part of the house.

"How much do you think you've got to have?"

"Two or three hundred dollars would see me through the fall and winter. Next spring we'll be able to get a big crop of cotton planted. All I need now is enough to see us through the fall and winter."

"I don't know if I can let you have that much. I tell you, I'm hard up myself right now. I've got some tenements downtown, but I can't collect much rent these days. I've had to put out seven or eight families already, and vacant rooms don't bring in a cent."

"Ask you wife for it then, son."

"When do you have to have it?"

"Right now. I need it to buy feed for the mules and rations for the household and two share-croppers. It takes a lot of money to run a farm these days when it's all going out and durn little coming in."

"I wish you could see me later. I'd be better fixed in another month. I've attached some furniture that ought to bring me in some money when it's sold. You don't know how hard up I am when I can't collect rent."

"I'm sorry to hear that you're selling poor people's household goods, son. That would make me ashamed of myself if I was you. I don't reckon I could bring myself to be so hard on my fellow-creatures."

"I thought you came here to borrow money. I can't stand here all night listening to your talk."

"Well, I've got to have some money, son," Ty Ty said. "Mules and share-croppers and my own household can't wait. We've got to eat, and eat quick."

Jim Leslie took out his pocketbook and counted an amount in ten- and twenty-dollar bills. He folded the money once and handed it to his father.

"That's a great help, son," Ty Ty said gratefully. "I sure do thank you from the bottom of my heart for helping me out at a time like this. When the nuggets come in, there won't be any need for borrowing more."

"That's all I can let you have. And don't come up to me on the street and ask for more. I can't let you have any more. You ought to stop trying to find gold out there and raise cotton and something to eat. There's no sense in a man with a hundred acres and two mules having to run to town every time he needs a bunch of beets. Raise it on the land out there. That's good land. It's been lying fallow, most of it, for twelve or fifteen years. Make those two share-croppers raise enough vegetables to feed themselves."

Ty Ty nodded his head at everything Jim Leslie said. He felt good now. The flat roll of money in his pocket raised him to a level with any man. Three hundred dollars was all he had wished for, and he had not expected to get any.

"I reckon we'll be going on home now," Ty Ty said.

Ty Ty went to the library and called Darling Jill and Griselda. They came into the hall and moved toward the door.

Jim Leslie was the last to leave the house. He followed them across the wide porch and down the steps to the walk. After they had seated themselves in Ty Ty's automobile, Jim Leslie came to the side where Griselda was and laid his hand on the door. He leaned against the car, looking at Griselda.

"Sometime when you're in town, come to see me," he said slowly, writing something on a card with his fountain pen and handing it to her. "I'm going to expect you, Griselda."

Griselda lowered her head to escape his eyes.

"I couldn't do that," she said.

"Why not?"

"Buck wouldn't like it."

"To hell with Buck," Jim Leslie said. "Come anyway. I'd like to talk to you."

"You'd better leave her alone and attend to your wife," Darling Jill said.

"I don't give a damn about her," he replied heatedly. "I'm going to look for you, Griselda."

"I can't do that," Griselda said again, shaking her head. "It wouldn't be fair to Buck. I'm his wife."

"I said to hell with Buck. I'm going to get you, Griselda. If you don't come to see me in my office the next time you're in town, I'm coming out there after you. Do you hear? I'm coming out there and bring you back here."

"Buck would shoot you, too," Darling Jill said. "He's had enough trouble with Will already."

"Will who? Who in hell is Will? What's he got to do with her?"

"You know Will Thompson."

"That lint-head? Good God, Griselda, you wouldn't let Will Thompson have anything to do with you, would you? That damn Horse Creek Valley lint-head?"

"What if he does live in a company town?" Darling Jill asked quickly. "He's a lot better than some of the people who live in these fine houses."

Jim Leslie put his arm over the back of the seat and dropped it closely around Griselda. She tried to move away from him, but he pulled her back. When she was still again, he leaned forward and tried to kiss her.

"You leave her alone, son, and let us be going home before trouble starts," Ty Ty said, standing up. "This here now pulling at her has got to stop."

"I'll drag her out of this damn automobile," he answered. "I know what I want."

Darling Jill started the car and it moved rapidly away. After it had gone several yards, Jim Leslie found that he could not remain there much longer. He knew Darling Jill might intentionally drive close to one of the trees along the curb and he would be knocked to the ground. He made one more effort to reach Griselda before he was forced from the runningboard. He reached for her, catching the open collar of her floral print frock in his fingers. He could feel the cloth suddenly give away, and he looked down at her and tried to see in the semidarkness. Before he could lean closer, Darling Jill swerved the car to the other side of the street, hurling him to the pavement.

He landed heavily on his hands and knees, but he was not so badly hurt as he thought he would be. The force of his fall made his hands and knees sting with pain, but he got to his feet immediately, brushing his clothes and watching the fast disappearing car in the distance.

At the next corner they all looked back and saw Jim Leslie standing under the street light dusting the dirt from his suit. There was a tear in the knee of one of his trousers legs, but he had not yet discovered it.

"I reckon you did the right thing," Ty Ty said, speaking to Darling Jill. "Jim Leslie didn't mean no harm to Griselda, but anything in God's world might have happened if he had kept on. He said something about dragging her out of the car, and he's man enough to do it, too. I'd hate, though, to have to leave here without her and have to face Buck downtown when he asked where she was."

"Oh, Jim Leslie is all right, Pa," Griselda said. "He didn't hurt me a bit. He didn't even scare me. He's too nice to be ugly."

"Well, it's mighty white of you to say that about him, but

I don't know. Jim Leslie is a Walden, and the Walden men ain't so well known for their timidity as they are for their getting what they're after. Maybe I'm wrong about that, though. Maybe I'm the only one with the name who's that way."

Coasting down the long steep grade to the brightly lighted city on the flood plain below, Ty Ty leaned forward to see what made Griselda's shoulders jerk so much. He could hear her trying to hold back sobs, but there were no tears in her eyes that he could see.

"Maybe Jim Leslie would have dragged her out, after all," he said to himself. "I don't know what else could be wrong with her, unless it is that. It takes a Walden to make the girls all wrought up."

He leaned further forward, crouching on his knees so he would not be hurled from the open car if Darling Jill should suddenly turn a corner while he was not expecting it. He looked forward and saw that Griselda was trying to fasten the tear in her new dress. It had been ripped down the front almost to her waist, exposing the creamy whiteness of her body. Ty Ty looked again before she pinned the dress securely together. He wondered if it had been anything he said that evening that was the cause of her dress being torn like that.

After a while he sat back on the seat, stretching his legs against the footrest, and clutched more tightly in his moist palm the roll of three hundred dollars Jim Leslie had let him have.

Chapter XIII

ROSAMOND, BUCK, AND SHAW were waiting on the downtown corner when they arrived. Will, though, was not in sight. They rode up to the curb and stopped, shutting off the motor. The second-storey windows behind the iron-grilled balconies were still open and lights were burning in most of them. Ty Ty tried not to look higher than the plate glass windows on the street level.

"Did you get it, Pa?" Rosamond asked, the first to reach the car.

"I reckon I did," he said proudly. "Just look at this big wad of greenbacks!"

Buck and Shaw were drawn to the side of the car to see it. Everyone looked pleased.

"I need a new raincoat," Shaw said.

"Son," Ty Ty said, shaking his head and pushing the roll of money back into his pocket out of sight, "son, when it rains, just peel off your clothes and let your skin take care of the rest. God never made a finer raincoat than a man's skin, anyhow."

"What are you going to do with all that money, Pa?" Buck said next. "You can spare a little of it, can't you? I haven't had any spending-money since a month ago Sunday."

"And you won't get none of this in a month of Sundays. You boys talk like this was nuggets I've got, expecting it to be shared. Jim Leslie let me have all this money to see us through the fall and winter. We've got to eat on this, and share with the mules besides."

Ty Ty craned his neck to find Will. He was anxious to leave for home, because it was nearly midnight then and he wished to get an early start in the morning. He was planning to resume digging at sunrise.

"Where's Will?"

"He was here a minute ago," Rosamond said, getting into the car and sitting down beside Ty Ty on the back seat. "He'll be back any second now."

"Will ain't gone and done it again, has he?" Ty Ty asked. "Ain't no sense in a man going to the dogs ever so often."

"Will didn't got to the dogs this time," Shaw said, winking at Griselda. "He went with a good-looking blonde. I reckon he's through with her by now, though, because the last time I saw him pass by he was getting ready to ditch her."

Rosamond choked back a sob.

"Will never means no harm," Ty Ty said. "Tomorrow morning bright and early we're all going to go out and get a good start digging in the holes. That'll straighten Will out."

"It looks like rain now," Shaw said. "Won't be no early start in the morning if it rains hard tonight."

"It can't rain now," Ty Ty said assuredly. "I'm against it raining for yet a while. We've got to dig in the holes without fail."

Each time there was a hard rain, the holes filled up with water, sometimes two or three feet deep. The only thing they could do in cases like that was to syphon it out with the long hose. They would put one end of the long hose in the hole they were digging, the other end in a hole situated lower on a

hillside, and syphon the water from one to the other. Before
Ty Ty had bought the second-hand fire hose from the Augusta
Fire Department, they had had many trying days of labor.
They had to carry out the water in buckets in those days, and
if the water was deep, a day or two was lost after every rain
before they could resume excavating the earth. With the fire
hose now they could syphon out several feet of water in an
hour or less.

Ty Ty continued to crane his neck, looking up the street
and down it.

"Here comes Will now."

Rosamond turned around to see in which direction Ty Ty
was looking. She began to sob again.

Will sauntered up to the car, his hat tilted precariously on
the side of his head, and leaned against the front mudguard
on Ty Ty's side. He took off his hat and fanned his face.

"Have any luck?" he shouted at Ty Ty. "Get the money,
fellow?"

He could be heard for several blocks. People as far away
as the next corner stopped and turned around and looked
back to see what the disturbance was.

"Hush, Will," Griselda said.

She was the closest to him and she believed it was her duty
to try to quiet him until they could get out of town.

"Why, hello there, good-looking!" Will shouted at her.
"Where'd you come from? I didn't see you when I drove up."

Buck and Shaw stood nearby and laughed at Will's be-
havior. The others were anxious to get him into the car and
drive away before a patrolman came by.

"I'm sure-God thankful I ain't a man of drinking habits,"
Ty Ty said. "Once I got started I wouldn't know when to stop.
I'd go the whole hog, as sure as God makes little green
apples."

Buck and Shaw helped Will into the back seat, in spite of
his violent protest. Rosamond pulled up the auxiliary seats
and gave Will her place beside Ty Ty. Buck sat with her while
Shaw and Ty Ty held Will down between them.

"You folks ain't doing me fair and square," Will protested,
kicking his feet against Ty Ty's shins. "I'm not getting justice.
Don't you know I can't leave the city till the last shot is fired?
Just look at everybody still up and walking the streets. Let me
out of here."

Darling Jill pulled away from the curb and started out the
street that led to the Marion highway.

"Now wait a minute," Will said. "Where we going? I'm

going home tonight. Turn around and take me to the Valley."

"We're going home, Will," Ty Ty said. "Now just sit back and cool off in the night air."

"That's a lie," he said, "because we're going toward Marion. I've got to get back to the Valley tonight. I've got to see about turning on the power in the mill."

"He's out of his head a little," Ty Ty said. "He drank too much raw corn."

"He talks about turning on the power even when he's sober, though," Rosamond said. "He even talks about it in his sleep at night now."

"Well, I don't know what he's talking about. I can't make head nor tail out of it. What power? What's he going to turn it on for?"

"Will says they're going to take the mill away from the company and turn on the power and run it themselves."

"That's just some more of those crazy cotton-mill workers' doings," Ty Ty said. "Farmers ain't never talking like that. Farmers are peace-loving creatures, taking it all in all. It looks like those fools in the Valley ain't got a bit of sense. Neither Will nor any of the rest of them. He ought to stay and farm some and dig a little in the holes on the side. I'm in favor of making him stay away from Horse Creek Valley before he gets his head shot off."

"He wouldn't be content to do that," Rosamond said. "I know Will. He's a loomweaver through and through. I don't suppose there ever was a man who loves a cotton mill as much as he does. Will talks about a loom just like it was a baby, sometimes. He wouldn't be content on a farm."

Will had stretched out on the seat, his feet propped against the footrest, and his head thrown back on top of the seat. He had not closed his eyes, however, and he looked as if he were aware of every word spoken.

They had left the city far behind. Each time they went over the crest of a sand hill they could look back and see the yellow glow of the lighted city behind them on the flood plain. Far up above it, looking as if it were built in the sky, the lighted streets of The Hill appeared like a castle in the clouds.

The big seven-passenger car was rushing through the night, its two long beams of light looking like the feelers of a fast flying insect as it broke through the wall of darkness ahead. Darling Jill had driven over the highway hundreds of times, and she knew when each curve was coming. The hot tires sang on the smooth concrete.

The fifteen miles to Marion were driven in twenty minutes.

Just before they reached the town, the car slowed down and they turned off the paved highway on the sand-clay road home. The house was only a mile and a half away, and they were there in a few minutes. Ty Ty got up reluctantly. He always enjoyed riding in an automobile at night.

"This has been my lucky day, folks," he said, climbing out and stretching. "Man alive! I feel like nobody's business!"

He walked over the yard, feeling the familiar hard white sand under his shoes. It was a wonderful sensation to come back home and walk around the yard. He liked to take trips to Marion and to Augusta merely for the opportunity it gave him to come back and walk over the hard white sand and to stand and look at the big piles of earth scattered over the farm like magnified ant hills.

Will sat up and stared at the shadowy outline of the house and barn. He rubbed his eyes and looked again, leaning forward in order to see better.

"Who brought me out here?" he asked. "I had to go home tonight."

"That's all right, Will," Rosamond said soothingly. "It was late, and Pa wanted to come home and go to bed. We'll get back tomorrow some way. If Darling Jill can't take us, we can go on the bus."

She put her arm around his waist and led him toward the house. He followed her resignedly.

"I'm going to turn the power on," he said.

"Of course you are, Will."

"If it's the last thing I ever do, I'm going to turn the power on."

"Of course, Will."

"They can't stop me. I'm going in there and throw those switches on, so help me God!"

"Let's go to bed now," Rosamond said tenderly. "When we get into bed, I'll rub your head and sing you to sleep."

They stumbled up the steps in the darkness and entered the house. Darling Jill and Griselda went behind them and lighted the lamps.

"I've been wondering how that Dave is," Ty Ty said. "Come on, boys, and we'll step down to the barn to see."

"I'm tired," Shaw said. "I want to go to bed."

"It won't take a minute, son. Just a minute."

They walked down to the barn silently. There was no moon, but the sky was clear and the stars were bright. The threatening clouds had disappeared, and there was little possibility of rain before morning. They went through the barn gate and on into the barn where the stalls were.

There was no sound, except that of somebody snoring. Even the mules were quiet.

Ty Ty struck a match and lighted the lantern that always hung by the barn door. He carried it to the stall where Dave slept at night.

"Well, I'll be a suck-egg mule," Ty Ty exclaimed in a low husky undertone.

"What's the matter, Pa?" Buck asked, coming up and looking through the hay rack.

"Now ain't that something, son?"

Shaw and Buck looked at Dave and at Uncle Felix. Both of them were sound asleep. Uncle Felix's shotgun was standing in the corner of the stall, and he was propped uncomfortably against the stall partition, with his head on his shoulder, snoring loud enough to be heard all the way to the other end of the barn. Dave had stretched out on his back and rested his head on a bundle of fodder. He looked as peaceful as a newborn babe, Ty Ty thought, and he turned away so Dave would not be disturbed.

"Don't bother them, boys," he said, backing off. "Uncle Felix couldn't help going to sleep. He looks dog-tired, sitting up there snoring to beat-the-band. And I don't reckon Dave is after getting loose. If he was, he'd be gone long before now. He's content to stay, it appears to me. Just leave them alone. He won't run off before morning, anyhow."

On the way back to the house, Buck walked beside his father.

"That Dave is after Darling Jill, Pa. You ought to stop him from taking up with her. The first thing you know, she'll be running off with him."

Ty Ty walked along thinking for several moments.

"He's already had her once," he said. "They went out under that oak tree yonder the other night, and that's where Will and me found them. What I'm thinking now is that I don't reckon I need to worry about them running off. A man and a girl only run off when they can't do what they're after at home. So I reckon there won't be nothing for them to run off together about. I've got a notion that Darling Jill is done with him, anyhow. She is set up all she wants."

Buck walked ahead a little distance. He spoke to his father over his shoulder. "You ought to make her behave herself, Pa. She's going to get ruined the way she's headed."

"Not if she keeps an eye on the curvature of the moon, she won't," he replied. "And I reckon Darling Jill can take care of herself all right. She knows what she's doing, most of the time. She's crazy as hell sometimes, and about nothing. But that don't keep her from knowing which is straight up and which is straight down."

Buck went into the house without further comment. Shaw went to the back porch for a drink of water before going to bed. Ty Ty was left in the hall alone.

The bedroom doors were open, and the rest of the house was getting ready for bed. Rosamond was undressing Will, pulling off his trousers by the cuffs while he sat on a chair falling asleep again. Ty Ty stood and watched them for several moments.

"See if you can't talk Will into staying here and working on the farm, Rosamond," he said, coming to the door. "I need somebody to oversee the crops. Me and the boys can't spare the time, because we've got to dig all the time, and those two darkies invite watching. They like to dig in their own holes better than they do plowing the crops."

"I couldn't make him do that, Pa," she said, shaking her head and looking up at Will. "It would break his heart if he had to leave the Valley and come over here to live. He's not made for farming and such things. He was raised in a mill town, and he's grown up in one. I couldn't think of trying to make him leave now."

Ty Ty walked away disappointed. He saw that it would be useless for the present to try to argue her into it.

At the door of Buck and Griselda's room he stopped and looked inside. They also were getting ready for bed. Buck was sitting on a chair taking off his shoes, and Griselda was sitting on the rug taking off her stockings.

They looked up when Ty Ty stopped at the door.

"What do you want, Pa?" Buck asked irritatedly.

"Son," he said, "I just can't help admiring Griselda, there. Ain't she the prettiest little girl you ever did see?"

Buck tossed his shoes and socks under the bed and lay down. He turned over, his back to Ty Ty, and pulled the sheet around his head.

Griselda shook her head at Ty Ty disapprovingly.

"Now, Pa," she said, looking up at him, "please don't start that now. You promised not to say that anymore, too."

Ty Ty put one foot inside the room and leaned against the door frame. He watched her roll and unroll her stockings and hang them over the back of the chair. She got up quickly and stood at the foot of the bed.

"You wouldn't begrudge me a little thing like that, now would you, Griselda?"

"Aw, now, Pa," she said.

Griselda waited for him to leave so she could finish undressing and put on her nightgown. Ty Ty waited in the doorway, one foot inside the room, admiring her. She finally began to unfasten her dress, glancing at him each moment. When she had unpinned it, she slipped her arms from the sleeves, holding it against her. With her other hand she put the nightgown over her head. Dexterously, she allowed the dress to drop to the floor while the nightgown slipped down over her shoulders and hips, but in the fraction of a second Ty Ty opened his eyes wider to see that there had been at least several inches between the top of the dress and the hem of the gown when they both slipped downward. He rubbed his eyes to see what had happened.

"Dog-gone my hide," he said, walking away into the dark hall. "Dog-gone it!"

Griselda blew out the light and jumped into bed.

Chapter XIV

IT LOOKED TO Ty Ty as if there would be trouble before evening. Since early that morning when they had started to work in the big hole beside the house, Buck had been uttering threats at Will, and Will had sat sullen and alone on the porch cursing Buck under his breath. All of them were digging, including Black Sam and Uncle Felix; everyone was working except Will, and he still refused to go down into the hole and shovel sand and clay in the hot sun.

Buck was in an ugly temper, and the increasing heat of midday in the hole, where there was not a breath of fresh air, made his anger more and more dangerous. All morning Ty Ty had done his best to keep Buck down there.

"I'll kill the son-of-a-bitch," Buck said for the fourth several time.

"Will ain't going to bother Griselda, Buck," Ty Ty told him. "Now go on and dig and leave him out of your mind."

Buck was not impressed by Ty Ty's assurances, even if

he did remain quiet for a while. Ty Ty climbed out of the hole to cool off a little. He got on top of the ground and looked around for Will, just to make sure that he was sitting peacefully on the front porch, cursing Buck under his breath.

Down in the crater. Dave was working with the rest. Ty Ty had come to the conclusion that the albino boy could be of greater service for the present if he would help dig. He had already divined the lode for Ty Ty, and Ty Ty thought it would be a good idea to let him help them strike it. The shotgun had been replaced on the rack in the dining-room, and he was no longer under guard. Uncle Felix had been singing that morning for the first time since Dave had been brought from the swamp. The colored man was glad to have the responsibility off his mind and to be allowed to dig with the rest of them.

When Ty Ty told Dave that he was not to be kept under guard any longer, the boy had acted as though he were afraid that Ty Ty would tell him to leave. When he was told to get down into the hole with Buck and Shaw, however, he was delighted. He had hoped that Darling Jill would come and talk to him, but she had not appeared. Dave was beginning to fear by that time that she was not going to have anything more to do with him. If she still cared for him, he believed she would have come to the crater and at least smiled at him.

"Will," Ty Ty said, sitting down and fanning himself with his straw hat, "what in the pluperfect hell do you boys want to scrap about, anyhow? That ain't no way for a family like us to be doing. I'm ashamed of the way you and Buck act."

"Listen," he answered quickly. "You tell him to keep his mouth shut, and you won't hear another word out of me. The only reason why I've ever said anything to him was because he's always calling me a lint-head, and saying he's going to kill me. Tell him to keep his mouth shut, and you won't be able to kick about what I say."

Ty Ty sat and thought a while. The mystery of human life was not nearly so obscure to him as it was to most men, and he wondered why everyone could not see as he did. Will Thompson probably came as close to understanding the secrets of the mind and body as he himself understood them, but Will was not the kind of man to tell what he knew. He went about his life keeping his thoughts to himself, and acting, when the time came, without revealing, save through his actions, the secrets of his knowledge. Ty Ty knew that the whole trouble between Will and Buck was over Griselda, and Buck was undoubtedly justified in being suspicious of Will's intentions.

Griselda was certainly not to blame for anything; she had never made an advance toward Will during the whole time she had been in the house. She always appeared to be trying so hard to keep Will away from her, and to make Buck believe that she cared only for him. Ty Ty knew she had had ample opportunity to deceive Buck if she had wished to; the truth was that she did not wish to deceive him. But she could not keep men from admiring her and being drawn to her and from trying to take her away from her husband. Ty Ty wondered what could be done about it.

"If there's one thing I've tried all my life to do, it's to keep peace in the family," he told Will. "I reckon I'd just fold up and die away if I saw blood spilled on my land. I'd never be able to get over the sight of it. I'd die to keep that from happening. I couldn't stand to see blood on my land."

"There's not going to be blood spilt, if Buck keeps his mouth shut and minds his own business. I've never tried to pick a fight with him. He always starts it, just like he started it this morning. I never even went close enough to him to say anything. He just came up and looked mean and started calling me a son-of-a-bitch and a lint-head, and the rest. That's all right with me. I don't intend to fight your boys for a little thing like that. But he keeps it up, rubbing it in all the time, and there's where the trouble is going to really start. If he'd say what it is he's got to say, and let it go with that, then it would be all right with me. But he hangs around saying it all day long. Tell him to shut up, if you don't want to see blood spilt on your land."

Ty Ty cocked his ears and listened. An automobile was slowing down to turn into the yard. Pluto Swint drove in and stopped under the shade of one of the live-oak trees. He got out laboriously, compressing his big round belly with the palms of his hands so he could squeeze himself between the door and the steeringwheel.

"I'm glad to see you, Pluto," Ty Ty said. He remained beside Will on the steps and waited for Pluto to come over and sit down. "I sure am glad to see you, Pluto. You got here just when I like to see you most. Somehow, it seems like you sort of bring a calming influence when you come. I can sit here now and feel satisfied that there won't be nothing to cause harm to me or mine."

Pluto blew and puffed and wiped his face free of perspiration, taking a seat on the steps. He looked at Will, nodding his head. Will spoke to him.

"Counted many votes today, so far?" Ty Ty asked.

"Not yet," Pluto answered, still blowing and puffing. "I couldn't get an early start today, and this is all the distance I've gone."

"Ain't it hot?"

"It's sizzling today," Pluto said. "And that's a fact."

Will took out his pocketknife and broke off a splinter on the steps and began whittling it. He could hear Buck saying something about him down in the hole around the house, but he was not interested in what he was saying.

"Me and Rosamond have got to go home today."

Ty Ty looked at him quickly, on the verge of protesting, but he held his tongue after a moment's thought. He wished to have Will there to help them dig, but Will would not dig, and he was of no help. That being the case, Ty Ty reasoned that it would be better for Will and Rosamond to go back to Scottsville. As long as Will remained there, Buck was going to make threats, and Will might not be so reasonable after another day. The safest and wisest course, Ty Ty said to himself, would be to let Will and Rosamond go home.

"I reckon we could have taken you last night when we were in Augusta," he said, "but it was pretty late, for one thing, and everybody wanted to come back and go to bed."

"I'll get Darling Jill to take us to Marion and we'll catch a bus. I've got to get back before night."

Ty Ty was relieved to think that perhaps there would be no trouble between Buck and Will after all. If they left soon, Buck would not have a chance to challenge Will.

"I'll go tell Darling Jill to get ready and drive you and Rosamond into town," he said rising.

"Sit down," Will told him, "and let's wait a while. There's no hurry. It's only about eleven o'clock now. We'll wait till after dinner."

Ty Ty sat down uneasily. The best he could hope for was that Will and Buck would not meet before then.

"How's politics now, Pluto?" he asked, trying to take his mind off such an unpleasant subject.

"Getting hot," Pluto said. "The candidates ain't content to count a vote once any longer; they're going out now and counting them over again to make sure they ain't lost them to somebody else. This running around all over the country has got me worn to a frazzle already. I don't see how I can keep up the chase like this for another six weeks."

"Now Pluto," Ty Ty said confidently, "you know you'll win in a walk. Every man I've talked with since New Year's Day has told me he was going to vote for you."

"Saying he's going to vote for me and doing it when the time comes is as far apart as the land and the sky. I don't put any trust in politics. I've been mixed up in them since I was twenty-two years old, and I know."

Ty Ty studied the smooth white sand in the yard, his eyes following the line of small round pebbles under the eaves of the porch where the water drained to the ground.

"I was just thinking, Pluto, that maybe you'd like to drive a little trip today."

"Where to?"

"Taking Will and Rosamond over to Horse Creek Valley in your car. I know the girls would be tickled to death to ride over there and back with you."

"I've got to be getting on down the road to count votes," Pluto protested. "And that's a fact."

"Now, you know you'd be pleased to ride over there and back, Pluto, carrying such fine-looking girls in your car. You ain't going to count votes sitting here in the yard, anyhow."

"I've got to get out and count votes all day long."

Ty Ty got up and went into the house, leaving Will and Pluto on the steps. Will rolled a cigarette and borrowed a match from Pluto. The sound of the pick striking the hard clay in the bottom of the crater around the house rose and fell in their ears to the rhythm of Uncle Felix's work-song. Pluto would have liked to have gone to the hole and looked down into it to see how deep it had been dug, but it was too much of an exertion for him to get up. He sat listening to the sound of the picks, trying to determine from the sound how deep the hole was. After he had thought about it a while, he was glad he had not gone around the house to look into it. He did not particularly care how deep it was, anyway; and, on top of that, if he had gone, the sight of seeing Buck and Shaw, the two darkies, and Dave sweating in the air-tight hole would have made him much hotter than he was already.

He looked up to see Darling Jill standing beside him. She was freshly dressed, swinging a wide-brimmed hat in her hands. She looked as if she were getting ready to go somewhere without consulting him. Will moved over a little and she sat down between them, putting her arm through Pluto's and placing her cheek against his shoulder.

"Pa said you were going to take Griselda and me for a ride to Scottsville," she smiled. "I didn't know anything about it until he came just now and told me."

Will laughed, leaning forward to see Pluto's face.

"I can't do that," Pluto protested.

"Now, Pluto, if you loved me a little you would."

"Well, I do that, anyway."

"Then you'll take us over with you when you take Will and Rosamond home."

"I've got to get out and count some votes," he said.

She reached up and kissed him on the cheek. Pluto beamed. He leaned closer so she would do it again.

"You can't be wasting your time canvassing for votes today, Pluto."

"I don't reckon I can," he said. "Can't you do that another time?"

"Once before we leave, and once before we start back," she promised.

"I sure can't get elected like this," Pluto said. "And that's a fact."

"There'll be plenty of time after today, Pluto."

She allowed his hand to rest on her knees, and watched him closely while he lifted her skirt and slipped his fingers under her garter.

"You're nothing but a big overgrown baby, Pluto. You're always wanting something you can't have."

"What do you say to getting married, Darling Jill?" he asked, his face flushing.

"It's not time yet."

"Why isn't it time yet?"

"Because I'd have to be a few months gone before I'd do that."

"It won't be long then," Will said, winking at Pluto.

Pluto was slow to understand what Darling Jill meant. He started to ask her, but he was silenced by Darling Jill's and Will's laughter.

"It won't be long if that fellow from the swamp stays here another week or so," Will said.

"Dave?" Darling Jill asked, making a face. "He's nothing. I wouldn't hurt Pa's little white-haired boy."

Pluto smiled contentedly when he heard her dismiss the albino so completely.

"Well, if you're going to forget him," Will said, "was I something, or wasn't I?"

"To tell the truth," she confessed, "you've got me worried."

"You ought to be. When I drive a nail into a plank, it stays driven."

"What's that you're talking about got to do with getting married, Darling Jill?" Pluto asked.

"Oh, nothing," she replied, winking at Will. "Will was just counting the daisies he picked."

"Well, I'm ready to get married," Pluto said.

"Well, I'm not," she said. "And that's a fact, too."

Will got up, laughing at Pluto, and went into the house to get ready to leave. Pluto put his arm around Darling Jill and hugged her. He knew he was going to drive them to Scottsville, because he would have done anything in the world Darling Jill asked. She sat close to him, submissive, while he squeezed her in his arms. She liked him, she knew she did. She thought she loved him, too, and in spite of his protruding stomach and his laziness. When the time came, she would marry him. She had already settled that much. What she did not know, was when the time would be.

Sitting so close to him then, she wished to tell him that she was sorry she had treated him so meanly at times, and had called him such vulgar names. When she turned to speak to him, however, she was afraid to say anything. She began to wonder of the wisdom of telling Pluto she was sorry she had been free with Will and Dave and with all the others while refusing him. She decided in that moment not to say anything about it, because it would not matter to him that she did not say it. She loved Pluto too much to see him hurt needlessly.

"Maybe next week we can get married, Darling Jill?"

"I don't know, Pluto. I'll tell you when I'm ready."

"I can't keep on waiting all the time," he said. "And that's a fact."

"But if you know you are going to marry me, you can wait a little while longer."

"That would be all right, maybe," he agreed, "if it wasn't that I'm scared somebody is going to come along and take you off some day."

"If I do go away with somebody, Pluto, I'll come back in time to marry you."

Pluto hugged her with both arms, trying to hold her so tightly that the impression of her body against his would be in his memory forever. She at last freed herself and stood up.

"It's time to leave, Pluto. I'll go get Will and Rosamond. Griselda ought to be ready by now."

Pluto walked out toward his car in the shade. He turned just in time to see Buck crawl out of the big hole and walk around the corner of the house. He met Griselda as she ran out the front door.

"Where are you going?" he demanded.

"Darling Jill and I are going to ride over to Scottsville with Pluto," she said, trembling. "We'll be back soon."

"I'll kill the son-of-a-bitch," he said, running up the steps.

Buck was angry and hot. His clay-soiled clothes and his perspiration-matted hair gave him the appearance of a man suddenly become desperate.

"Please, Buck," she begged.

"Where is he now?"

She tried to talk to Buck, but he would not listen to her. Just then Ty Ty came out of the house and took Buck by the arm.

"You'd better leave me alone, now," he told Ty Ty.

"Let the girls go for the ride, Buck. There ain't no harm in that."

"You'd better turn me loose, now."

"It's all right, Buck," Ty Ty argued. "Darling Jill and Rosamond will be along, and Pluto in the car, too. Let the girls go along for the ride. Can't no harm come of that."

"I'll kill the son-of-a-bitch, now," Buck said unchanged. He was not impressed by his father's assurance of Griselda's safety.

"Buck," Griselda begged, "please don't be angry. There's nothing to talk like that about."

Ty Ty led him down the steps into the yard and tried to talk with him.

"You'd better leave me alone, now," he said again.

They began walking up and down in the yard, Ty Ty leading him by the arm. After a while, Buck pulled away and went back to the crater beside the house. He was not so angry as he had been, and not nearly so hot, and he was willing to go back to work and let Griselda go in the car to Scottsville. He went back where Shaw and Dave and the two colored men were without saying another word.

When they were certain Buck had gone to the crater to stay, Darling Jill and Rosamond stopped holding Will in the house and allowed him to come out and get into the car.

Chapter XV

THEY REACHED SCOTTSVILLE in the upper end of the Valley two hours later.

Will had jumped out of the car when they stopped in front of the house and had run down the street, shouting back over his shoulder for them to stay until he came home. That had been in the middle of the afternoon, and at six he had not returned.

Pluto was anxious to get back to Georgia, and Griselda was frantic. She did not know what Buck might do to her for not returning home immediately, and it frightened her to think about it. She was glad to stay as long as she could, though, because it was the first time she had ever been in Horse Creek Valley, and the feeling of the company town gave her a pleasure she had never before experienced. The rows of yellow company houses, all looking alike to the eye, were individual homes to her now. She could look into the yellow company house next door and almost hear the exact words the, people were saying. There was nothing like that in Marion. The houses in Marion were buildings with closed doors and uninviting windows. Here in Scottsville there was a murmuring mass of humanity, always on the verge of filling the air with a concerted shout.

Pluto and Darling Jill had made a freezer of ice cream while they were waiting for Will to come home. At dark when he still had not returned, they ate the cream with graham crackers for the evening meal. Pluto was still restless, wishing to get back to Georgia. He felt uncomfortable in Horse Creek Valley and he did not like to think too much of the probability of being there long after dark. For some reason he was suspicious of cotton mill towns, and firmly believed that after dark people came out of hiding and preyed upon strangers, robbing them and beating them if not actually murdering them.

"I really believe Pluto is scared to go out of the house after dark," Darling Jill said.

Pluto trembled at the suggestion, clutching his chair. He was afraid, and if one of them asked him to go to a store down the street on an errand he would refuse to leave the house. At home in Marion he was afraid of nothing; the darkness of

113

night had never cowed him before in all his life. But here in the Valley he trembled with acute fear; he did not know at what minute somebody would run through the unlocked door and strike him dead in his tracks.

"Will can't possibly stay out much longer," Rosamond said. "He always comes home for supper at night."

"I wish we could go, anyway," Griselda said. "Buck will be wild."

"Both of you are scared to death," Darling Jill laughed. "There's nothing to be scared of here, is there, Rosamond?"

Rosamond laughed. "Of course not."

Through the open windows the soft summer night floated into the room. It was a soft night, and it was warm; but with the evening air there was something else that excited Griselda. She could hear sounds, voices, murmurs that were like none she had ever heard before. A woman's laughter, a child's excited cry, and the faint gurgle of a waterfall somewhere below all came into the room together; there was a feeling in the air of living people just like herself, and this she had never felt before. The new knowledge that all those people out there, all those sounds, were as real as she herself was made her heart beat faster. Never had the noises of Augusta sounded like these; in the city there were other sounds of another race of people. Here in Scottsville the people were as real as she herself was at that moment.

Will came in then, surprising her, and walked as noiselessly as a soft-toed animal. Griselda felt like running to him and throwing her arms around his neck when she first saw him. He was one of the persons she had felt in the night air.

He stood in the door of the room looking at them.

There was a look on Will's face that forced Griselda to suppress a cry that rose to her throat. She had never seen an expression on anyone's face such as he had. There was a painful plea in his eyes, a look that she had seen wounded animals have. And the lines of his face, the position of his head on his shoulders, something, whatever it was, was horrifying to look upon.

He seemed to be trying to say something. He looked as if he were bursting with words that he could not turn loose. All the things she had ever heard Rosamond say about the cotton mill down there below were written on his face more plainly than human words could express.

Will was speaking to Rosamond. His lips moved in the form of words long before she heard them. It was like looking through a pair of binoculars at a man speaking afar off, and seeing his lips move before the sound reached her ears. She looked at him wild-eyed.

"We had the meeting," he told Rosamond. "But they wouldn't listen to Harry and me. They voted to arbitrate. You know what that means."

"Yes," Rosamond said simply.

Will turned and looked at Griselda and the others.

"So we're going ahead and do it anyway. To hell with the damn local. They draw pay for arguing with us. To hell with them. We're going to turn the power on."

"Yes," Rosamond said.

"I'll be damned if I sit still and see them starve us with a dollar-ten, and charging rent on what we live in. There are enough of us to get in there and turn the power on. We can run the damn mill. We can run it better than anybody else. We're going down there in the morning and turn it on."

"Yes, Will," his wife said.

A light was switched on in one of the rooms of the yellow company house next door.

"We're going to turn the power on, and I'm man enough to do it. You'll see. I'm as strong as God Almighty Himself is now. You'll hear about the power being turned on tomorrow. Everybody will hear about it."

He sat down in silence and buried his head in his hands. No one spoke. He was the one to speak, if anyone did.

A darkness enveloped everything. For a while the whole memory of his life passed across his eyes. He squeezed the lids over the eyeballs, straining to forget the memory. But he could not forget. He could see, dimly at first, the mills in the Valley. And while he looked, everything was as bright as day. He could see, since the time he could first remember, the faces of the wild-eyed girls like morning-glories in the mill windows. They stood there looking out at him, their bodies firm and their breasts erect, year after year since he could first remember being alive. And out in the streets in front of the mills stood bloody-lipped men, his friends and brothers, spitting their lungs into the yellow-dust of Carolina. Up and down the Valley he could see them, count them, call them by their names. He knew them; he had always known them. The men stood in the streets watching the ivy-covered mills. Some of them were running night and day, under blinding blue lights; some of them were closed, barred against the people who starved in the yellow company houses. And then the whole

Valley was filled with the people who suddenly sprang up. There again were the girls with eyes like morning-glories and breasts so erect, running into the ivy-covered mills; and out in the street, day and night, stood his friends and brothers, looking, and spitting their lungs into the yellow dust at their feet. Somebody turned to speak to him, and through his parted lips issued blood instead of words.

Will shook his head, hitting the sides of it with the heel of his hands, and looked around him in the room. Pluto and Darling Jill, Griselda and Rosamond, were looking at him. He drew the back of his hand over his mouth, wiping away the dried blood and the warm blood he thought he felt on his lips.

"I told you to stay till I got back, didn't I?" he said, looking steadily at Griselda.

"Yes, Will."

"And you stayed. Thank God for that."

She nodded.

"We're going to turn the power on the first thing in the morning. That's settled. We're going to do that, no matter what happens."

Rosamond looked at him anxiously. She believed for a moment that he was out of his mind. It was something in the way he spoke, something that sounded strange in his voice; she had never heard him talk like that before.

"Are you all right, Will?" she asked.

"Oh, God, yes," he said.

"Try not to think so much about the mill tonight. It will make you so restless you won't be able to go to sleep."

Murmurs passed through the company streets of the company town, coming in rhythmic tread through the windows of the company house. It was alive, stirring, moving, and speaking like a real person. Griselda felt her heart ache with sharp pain.

"You've never worked in a spinning mill, have you, Pluto?" he asked suddenly, turning upon Pluto.

"No," he answered weakly. "I've got to be getting back home right away."

"You don't know what a company town is like, then. But I'll tell you. Have you ever shot a rabbit, and gone and picked him up, and when you lifted him in your hand, felt his heart pounding like—like, God, I don't know what! Have you?"

Pluto stirred uneasily in his chair. He turned to look at Griselda beside him and saw a convulsive shiver envelop her.

"I don't know," Pluto said.

"God!" Will murmured hoarsely.

They looked at him, trembling, all of them. Somehow, they had felt exactly what he had meant when he said that. They were frightened by the revelation.

A new murmur passed through the company house, floating softly through row after row of other yellow company houses.

"You think I'm drunk, don't you?" he asked.

Rosamond shook her head. She knew he was not.

"No, I'm not drunk. I've never been as sober as I am now. You think I'm drunk because I talk like that. But I'm sober, as sober as a stick of wood."

Rosamond said something to him, something tenderly soft and understanding.

"Back there in Georgia, out there in the middle of all those damn holes and piles of dirt, you think I'm nothing but a dead sapling sticking up in the ground. Well, maybe I am, over there. But over here in the Valley, I'm Will Thompson. You come over here and look at me in this yellow company house and think that I'm nothing but a piece of company property. And you're wrong about that, too. I'm Will Thompson. I'm as strong as God Almighty Himself now, and I can show you how strong I am. Just wait till tomorrow morning and walk down the street there and stand in front of the mill. I'm going up to that door and rip it to pieces just like it was a window shade. You'll see how strong I am. Maybe you'll go back to those God damn pot holes in Marion and think a little different after tomorrow."

"You'd better go to bed now, Will, and get some sleep. You'll have to get up early in the morning."

"Sleep! To hell with sleep! I'm not going to sleep now, or any time tonight. I'll be as wide awake when the sun rises as I am now."

Pluto wished to be able to get up and leave, but he was afraid to say anything while Will was talking. He did not know what to do. He looked at Darling Jill and at Griselda, but neither of them seemed anxious to go home now. They sat enthralled before Will.

Griselda sat before Will looking up at him as if he were a precious idol come to life. She felt like getting down on the floor in front of him and throwing her arms around his knees and begging for the laying of his hand on her head.

He was looking at her when she found the courage to look up. He was looking at her as if he had never seen her before.

"Stand up, Griselda," he said calmly.

She stood up immediately, rising eagerly at his command. She waited for anything he might tell her to do next.

"I've waited a long time for you, Griselda, and now is the time."

Rosamond made no move to speak or to get up. She sat calmly in her chair, her hands folded in her lap, waiting to hear what he would say the next moment.

"Ty Ty was right," Will said.

All of them wondered what Will meant. Ty Ty had said many things, so many things that it was impossible for them to know what Will had in mind.

But Griselda knew. She knew precisely the words he had used and to which Will now referred.

"Before you go any further, Will," Darling Jill said, "you'd better not forget Buck. You know what he said."

"He said he would kill me, didn't he? Well, why doesn't he come and do it? He had the chance to try it this morning. I was over there among those God damn pot holes. Why didn't he do it then?"

"He can still do it. There'll be time enough for it."

"I'm not scared of him. If he ever makes a move at me, I'll twist his neck off and throw it into one of those God damn pot holes, and him into another."

"Will," Rosamond said, "please be careful. Buck can't be stopped once he sets his head on doing something. If you put your hands on Griselda, and Buck ever hears about it, he'll kill you as sure as the world we stand on."

He was no longer interested in hearing them express their fear of what Buck would do.

Griselda stood before him. Her eyes were closed and her lips were partly open, and her breath came rapidly. When he told her to sit down, she would sit down. Until then she would remain standing for the rest of her life.

"Ty Ty was right," Will said, looking at her. "He knew what he was talking about. He told me about you, lots of times, but I didn't have sense enough to take you then. But I'm going to now. Nothing in God's world can stop me now. I'm going to have it, Griselda. I'm as strong as God Almighty Himself now, and I'm going to do it."

Darling Jill and Pluto moved nervously in their seats, but Rosamond sat calmly quiet with folded hands in her lap.

"I'm going to look at you like God intended for you to be seen. I'm going to rip every piece of those things off of you in a minute. I'm going to rip them off and tear them into pieces so small you'll never be able to put them together again. I'm going to rip the last damn thread. I'm a loomweaver. I've woven cloth all my life, making every kind of fabric in God's world. Now I'm going to tear all that to pieces so small nobody will ever know what they were. They'll look like lint when I get through. Down there in the mill I've woven ginghams and shirting, denim and sheeting, and all the rest; up here in this yellow company house I'm going to tear hell out of the cloth on you. We're going to start spinning and weaving again tomorrow, but tonight I'm going to tear that cloth on you till it looks like lint out of a gin."

He went toward her. The veins on the backs of his hands and around his arms swelled and throbbed, looking as if they would burst. He came closer, stopping at arm's length to look at her.

Griselda stepped backward out of his reach. She was not afraid of Will, because she knew he would not hurt her. But she stepped backward out of his reach, afraid of the look in his eyes. Will's eyes were not cruel, and they were not murderous—he would not hurt her for anything in the world—they were too tender for that now—and his eyes were coming closer and closer.

Will caught the collar of her dress, a hand on each side, and flung his arms wide apart. The thin printed voile disintegrated in his hands like steam. He had ripped it from her, tearing it insanely in his hands, quickly, eagerly, minutely. She watched him with throbbing excitement, following the arcs of his flying fingers and the motions of his arms. Piece by piece he tore like a madman, hurling the fluffy lint in all directions around the room when he bent forward over the cloth. She watched him unresistingly when he flung the last of the dress aside and ripped open the white slip as though it were a paper bag. He was working faster all the time, tearing, ripping, jerking, throwing the shredded cloth around him and blowing the flying lint from his face. The final garment was silk. He tore at it frantically, even more savagely than he had at the beginning. When that was done, she was standing before him, waiting, trembling, just as he had said she would stand. Perspiration covered his face and chest. His breathing was difficult. He had worked as he had never done before, and the shredded cloth lay on the floor at his feet, covering them.

"Now!" he shouted at her. "Now! God damn it, now! I told you to stand there like God intended for you to be seen! Ty Ty was right! He said you were the most beauti-

ful woman God ever made, didn't he? And he said you were
so pretty, he said you were so God damn pretty, a man would
have to get down on his hands and knees and lick something
when he saw you like you are now. Didn't he? Yes, so help
me God, he did! And after all this time I've got you at last, too.
And I'm going to do what I've been wanting to do ever since
the first time I saw you. You know what it is, don't you,
Griselda? You know what I want. And you're going to give it
to me. But I'm not like the rest of them that wear pants.
I'm as strong as God Almighty Himself is now. And I'm going
to lick you, Griselda. Ty Ty knew what he was talking about.
He said that was what a man would do to you. He's even got
more sense than all the rest of us put together, even if he does
dig in the ground like a God damn fool."

He paused for breath, going toward her. Griselda backed
toward the door. She was not trying to escape from him now,
but she had to go away from him until he caught her and
dragged her to another part of the house. He ran, throwing his
hands on her.

Chapter XVI

FOR A LONG TIME after they had gone Darling Jill sat squeezing
her fingers with savage excitement. She was afraid to look
across the room at her sister then. The beating within her
breast frightened her, and she was almost choked with nerv-
ousness. Never before had she felt so completely aroused.

But when she did not look at her sister, she was afraid
of being alone. She turned boldly and looked at Rosamond,
and she was surprised to see such composure as Rosamond
possessed. She was rocking a little in the chair, folding her
hands and unfolding them without haste. There was an expression of sereneness on Rosamond's face that was beautiful
to behold.

Beside her, Pluto was bewildered. He had not felt the things
she had. She knew no man would. Pluto was speechless with
wonder at Will and Griselda, but he was unmoved. Darling
Jill had felt the surge of their lives pass through the room
while Will stood before them tearing Griselda's clothes to
shreds, and Rosamond had. But Pluto was a man, and he would
never understand how they felt. Even Will, who brought it,
had acted only with the guidance of his want of Griselda.

Through the open doors they could see the restless flicker of the street light breaking through the leaves of the trees and falling on the bed and floor of the room. Over there, in that room, were Will and Griselda. They were not in hiding, because the doors were open; they were not in secret, because their voices were strong and distinct.

"I'll pick up some of the lint now," Rosamond said calmly. She got down on her knees and began gleaning the minute particles of cotton fiber from the floor, piling them carefully beside her. "I don't need any help."

Darling Jill watched her while she gathered the threads and torn cloth slowly and with care. She bent over, her face obscured, and picked piece by piece the clothes torn from Griselda. When she had finished, she went to the kitchen and brought back a large paper bag. Into it she placed the torn voile and underclothing.

It seemed to Darling Jill that Will and Griselda had been in the room across the hall for hours. They no longer were talking, and she began to wonder if they had gone to sleep. Then she remembered that Will had said he would not sleep that night, and she knew he would be awake even if Griselda were not. She waited for Rosamond to return from the kitchen.

Rosamond came back and sat down across from her.

"Buck is going to kill Will when he hears about this," Darling Jill said.

"Yes," Rosamond replied. "I know."

"He'll never find out from me, but he'll learn of it in some way. Maybe he'll just feel it or something. But he will certainly know what happened."

"Yes," Rosamond said.

"He may be on his way over here now. He expected Griselda to come straight back."

"I don't believe he will come tonight. But he may come to-morrow."

"Will ought to go away somewhere, so Buck won't be able to find him."

"No. Will wouldn't go anywhere. He'll stay here. We couldn't make him leave."

"But Buck will kill him, Rosamond. If he stays here, and Buck hears about it, he'll be killed as sure as the world. I'm certain of that."

"Yes," Rosamond said. "I know."

Rosamond went to the kitchen to see what time it was by the clock. It was between three and four in the morning then. She came back and sat down, folding her hands and unfolding them without haste.

"Aren't we ever going home?" Pluto asked.

"No," Darling Jill said. "Shut up."

"But I've got to——"

"No, you haven't. Shut up."

Will appeared noiselessly at the door, barefooted. He was wearing only a pair of khaki pants, and he looked like a loom-weaver, bare-backed and sleep-refreshed, ready to go to work.

He sat down in the room with them, holding his hands around his head. He had the appearance of someone trying to protect his head from an enemy's fists.

Darling Jill felt the returning surge of savage excitement grip her. She could never again look at Will without that feeling coming over her. The memory of seeing Will stand in front of Griselda tearing her clothes to threads like a madman, hearing him talk like Ty Ty, watching him clutch Griselda with swollen muscles, that memory was branded upon her as if it had been seared upon her body with white-hot irons. She stood it as long as she could, and then she ran and fell at his feet, hugging his knees and kissing him all over. Will laid his hands on her head and stroked her hair.

She stirred jerkily, rising to her knees and thrusting her body between his legs, and locked her arms around his waist. Her head was buried against him, and she hugged him with her arms and shoulders. It was only when she could find his hands that she lay still against him. One after the other she kissed his fingers, pushing them between her lips and into her mouth. But after that, she still was not satisfied.

He continued to stroke her hair, slowly and heavily. His head was thrown back and his other arm was thrown around his face and forehead.

"What time is it?" he asked after a while.

Rosamond got up and went again to the kitchen and looked at the clock.

"It's twenty past four, Will," she said.

He covered his face again, trying to blot out the light from his eyes. His mind was so clear he could follow a thought through the endless tube of his brain. Each thought reached to endless depths, but each time it returned after the whirling journey of his brain. Each thought raced around and around in his head, flowing smoothly from cell to cell, and he closed his eyes and knew at each moment the exact point on his skull where he could place the tip of his finger and locate it.

Up and down the Valley his mind raced, biting eagerly at the doors of the yellow company houses and at the windows of the ivy-walled mills. At Langley, at Clearwater, at Warrenville, at Bath, at Graniteville, he stopped for a moment to look at the people going into the spinning mills, the bleacheries, the weaving mills.

He came back to the room in the yellow company house in Scottsville and listened to the early morning hum of motor trucks and trailers and the whirr of passenger cars and busses on the Augusta-Aiken highway speeding over the wide concrete up and down the Valley. When the sun rose, he would be able to see the endless regiments of wild-eyed girls with erect breasts, firm-bodied girls who looked like morning-glories through the windows of the ivy-walled mills. But out in the streets, in the early morning shadow of the sun, he would see the endless rows of bloody-lipped men, his friends and brothers standing with eyes upon the mills, spitting their lungs into the yellow dust of Carolina.

At sunrise, in the cool black-and-white of morning, Griselda came to the door. She had not been asleep. She had lain upon the bed in the other room prolonging with bated breath the night that so inevitably merged into day. It was day now, and the red glow of the sun rising over the house-tops covered her with a glow of warmth that flushed her face again and again while she stood in the doorway.

Rosamond got up.

"I'll cook breakfast now, Will," she said.

They went out, the three of them, going first to one of the other rooms to clothe Griselda.

Later in the kitchen Will heard them at the table and at the stove. First there was the smell of chewed grain, the boiling grits; then the smell of frying meat, the hunger for food; and finally there was the smell of coffee, the start of a new day.

Through the window he could see someone in the kitchen of the yellow company house next door making a fire in the cook-stove. Soon there came the curl of blue wood smoke from the chimney top. People were getting up early today; for the first time in eighteen months the mill was going to run. Down at the mill beside cool, broad, dammed-up Horse Creek they were going to turn on the power. The machinery would turn, and men would be standing in their places, stripped to the waist, working again.

He went to the kitchen impatiently. He wished to fill his stomach with warm food and to run down the street calling to his friends in the yellow company houses on both sides of the street. They would come to the door, shouting to him. On the way down to the mill the mass of men would grow, piling into the green in front of the mill, chasing away the sheep that had grazed so fat for eighteen months while men and women and children had grown hollow-eyed on grits and coffee. The barb-wire steel fence would be up-rooted, the iron posts and the concrete-filled holes would be raised into the air, and the first bar would be lowered.

"Sit down, Will," Rosamond said.

He sat down at the table, watching them prepare a place for him hurriedly, easily, lovingly. Darling Jill brought a plate, a cup, and a saucer. Griselda brought a knife, a spoon, and a fork. Rosamond filled a glass of water. They ran over the kitchen, jumping from each other's way, weaving in and out in the small room hurriedly, easily, lovingly.

"It's six o'clock," Rosamond said.

He turned and looked at the face of the clock on the shelf over the table. They were going to turn the power on that morning. They were going in there and turn it on and if the company tried to shut it off, they were going to—well, God damn it, Harry, the power is going to stay turned on.

"Here's the sugar," Griselda said.

She put two spoonfuls into the coffee cup. She knew. It wasn't every woman who would know how much sugar to put into his cup. She's got the finest pair of rising beauties a man ever laid eyes on, and when you once see them, you're going to get right down on your hands and knees and lick something. Ty Ty has got more sense than all of us put together, even if he does stay out there among those God damn pot holes digging for what he'll never find.

"I'll bring a dish for the ham," Darling Jill said.

Rosamond stood behind his chair, watching him cut the meat and place hungry bites into his mouth. It was the thirty-pound ham Ty Ty had given them.

"What time will you be home for lunch?" she asked.

"Twelve-thirty."

Already men were walking down the street towards the ivy-walled mill by the side of broad Horse Creek. Men who had all night, sitting at windows, looking at the stars, left as soon as they had finished breakfast, walking down the street towards the mill in khaki pants. No one looked at the ground on which he walked. Down at the ivy-walled mill the windows reflected the early morning sun, throwing it upon the yellow company houses and into the eyeballs of men walking down the streets. We're going in there and turn the power on and if the company tries to shut it off—well, God damn it, Harry, it's going to stay turned on.

"Could you get us jobs in the mill, Will?" Darling Jill asked him. "For Buck and Shaw and me?"

He shook his head.

"No," he said.

"I wish you would, Will, so we could move over here."

"This is no place for you, or the others."

"But you and Rosamond live here."

"That's different. You stay in Georgia."

He shook his head again and again.

"I wish I could come," Griselda said.

"No," he said.

Rosamond brought him his shoes and socks. She knelt on the floor at his feet, putting them on his feet. He worked his shoes on and she tied them. Then she got up and stood behind his chair.

"It's nearly seven o'clock," she said.

He looked up at the clock above. The minute hand was between ten and eleven.

People passed the yellow company house faster, all going swiftly in one direction. Women and children were among them. The local draws pay for sitting on their tails on the platform and shaking their heads when somebody says something about turning the power on. The sons-of-bitches. The union sends money in here to pay those sons-of-bitches who run the local, and the rest of us grow hollow-eyed on grits and coffee. The people were walking faster down the street, their eyes on a level with the sun-red mill windows. Nobody looked down at the ground on which he walked. Their eyes were on the sun-bright windows of the ivy-walled mill. The children ran ahead, looking up at the windows.

Somebody came through the house and into the kitchen. He found and jerked a chair. He sat down beside Will, his head a little on one side, his other hand on the back of Will's chair. He watched Will Thompson eat grits and ham. Where'd you get the ham, Will? Jesus Christ, it looks good!

"They've brought down some plain-clothes guards from the Piedmont, Will."

"When did you find that out, Mac?"

He swallowed the ham unchewed.

"I saw them when they got here. I was just getting up, and

I looked out the window and saw three cars of them drive
around to the rear of the mill. You can tell those bastards
from the Piedmont a mile off."

Will got up and went to the front of the house. Mac followed him, his eyes sweeping the girls as he left. They could
be heard talking in the front room where Pluto was asleep in
the chair.

Griselda began washing the dishes. None of them had eaten
anything. But they drank coffee while they washed the dishes
and tried to hurry. There was no time to waste. They had to
hurry.

"We ought to start back home, but I would rather stay,"
Griselda said.

"We are going to stay," Darling Jill said.

"Buck might come."

"He will come," Rosamond said. "We can't stop him."

"I'm sorry," Griselda said.

They knew without asking further what she meant.

"I would rather you wouldn't be. I wish you wouldn't say
that. I'd rather that you weren't sorry."

"It's all right, Griselda," Darling Jill spoke. "I know Rosamond better than you do. It's all right."

"If Buck ever finds out about it, he'll kill Will," Rosa-
mond said. "That's all I'm sorry about. I don't know what
I would do without Will. But I know Buck's going to kill him.
I'm certain of it. Nothing can stop him when he finds it out."

"But there is something we can do, isn't there?" Griselda
said. "I couldn't let that happen. It would be awful."

"I don't know anything to do. I'm afraid Pluto might say
something when he gets back, too."

"I'll attend to him," Darling Jill promised.

"But you never can tell what may happen. If Buck asks
him a question, he can read his face. Pluto couldn't hide anything."

"I'll talk to Pluto before we get back. He'll be careful after
I get through talking to him."

They went into the front of the house. Pluto was still asleep,
and Will and Mac had left. They began getting ready quickly.

"Oh, let Pluto sleep," Darling Jill said.

Griselda put on some of Rosamond's clothes. She had her
own slippers. Rosamond's dress looked well on her. They
each stopped and admired it.

"Where's Will gone to?" Darling Jill asked.

"To the mill."

"We've got to hurry. They're going to turn the power on."

"It's nearly eight o'clock. They may not wait much longer. We can't wait any longer."

They ran out of the house, one behind the other. Down the street they ran towards the ivy-walled mill trying to keep together in the crowd. Everyone's eyes were on a level with the windows that the sun shone so redly upon.

"Buck will kill him," Griselda said, breathless.

"I know it," said Rosamond. "We can't stop him."

"He'll have to shoot me too, then," Darling Jill cried. "When he points a gun at Will, I'll be the first to be shot. I would rather die with Will than live after he was killed by Buck. Buck will have to shoot me."

"Look!" Rosamond cried, pointing.

They stopped, raising their heads above the crowd. Men were gathering around the company fence. The three sheep so fat that had grazed on the green for eighteen months were being chased away. The fence was raised into the air—iron posts, concrete holes, and the barb-wire and steel mesh.

"Where's Will?" Griselda cried. "Show me Will!"

Chapter XVII

"THERE THEY GO!" Rosamond said, clutching the arms of her sister and Griselda. "Will is at the door now!"

Women all around them were crying hysterically. After eighteen months of waiting it looked as if there would again be work in the mill. Women and children pushed forward, stronger than the force of the walled-up water in Horse Creek below, pushing close behind the men at the mill door. Some of the older children had climbed up the trees and they were above the crowd now, hanging to the limbs and shouting at their fathers and brothers.

"I can't believe it's true," a woman beside them said. She had stopped crying long enough to speak.

All around them women and girls were crying with joy. When the men had first said they were going to take over the mill and turn on the power, the women had been afraid; but now, now when they were crushed against the mill, it looked as if everything would come true. Here in the mill yard now were the mild-eyed Valley girls with erect breasts;

behind the mill windows they would look like morning-glories.

"It's open!" somebody shouted.

There was a sudden surge of closely pressed bodies, and Rosamond and Darling Jill and Griselda were pushed forward with the mass.

"We'll have something beside fat-back and Red Cross flour now," a little woman with clenched fists said in a low voice beside them. "We've been starving on that, but we won't any longer. The men are going to work again."

Already the mass of men were pouring through the opened doors. They fought their way in silently, hammering at the narrow doors with their fists and pushing them with their muscles, angry because the doors were not wide enough to admit them quicker. Windows on the first floor were being tilted open. The crowd of women and children could follow the advance of the men by watching the opening of the mill windows one after the other. Before the first floor windows were all opened, several on the second floor were suddenly tilted wide.

"There they are," Rosamond said. "I wonder where Will is now."

Somebody said that the company had hired fifteen additional guards and placed them in the mill. The new guards had arrived that morning from the Piedmont.

The entire mill was occupied. The third and fourth floor windows were being opened. Already men were running to the windows on all floors, jerking off their shirts and flinging them to the ground. When men in the Valley went back to work after a long lay-off, they took off their shirts and threw them out the windows. Down on the green, where the three company sheep so fat had grazed for eighteen months, the ground was covered with shirts. The men on the last two floors were throwing out their shirts, and down on the ground the piled shirts were knee deep on the green.

"Hush!" the whisper went over the crowd of women and girls and yelling children in the trees.

It was time for the power to be turned on. Everyone wished to hear the first concerted hum of the machinery behind the ivy-walled building.

"I wonder where Will is," Rosamond said.

"I haven't seen him at the window yet," Griselda said. "I've been looking for him."

Darling Jill stood on her toes, straining to see over the heads of the people. She clutched Rosamond, pointing to a window above.

"Look! There's Will! See him at the window?"

"What's he doing?"

"He's tearing his shirt to pieces!" Rosamond cried.

They stood on their toes trying their best to see Will before he left the window.

"It is Will!" Griselda said.

"Will!" Darling Jill cried, urging all the strength of her body into her lungs so he might hear her above the noise. "Will! Will!"

For a moment they thought he had heard her. He stopped and bent far out the window trying to see down into the tensely packed mass below. With a final tear he balled the ripped cloth in his hands and threw it out into the crowd. The women nearest the mill reached up and fought for the worn strips of cloth. The ones who caught parts of it quickly took it from the reach of the others who wished to have a part of it.

Rosamond and Darling Jill and Griselda could not get close enough to fight for Will's torn shirt. They had to stand where they were and see the other women and girls struggle over it until there was none left.

"Let's hear the machinery, Will Thompson!" an excited woman cried.

"Turn the power on, Will Thompson!" another girl cried at him.

He turned and ran out of sight. The crowd below was as still as the empty mill yard had been before they came. They waited to hear the first hum of the machinery.

Rosamond's heart beat madly. It was Will whom the crowd begged to turn the power on. It was he whom they had acknowledged by acclamation as their leader. She wished to climb up high above the mass of crying women and shout that Will Thompson was her husband. She wished to have all the people there know that Will Thompson was her Will.

Through the tilted glass windows they could see the men at their places, waiting for the wheels to turn. Their voices were raised in shouts that burst through the windows, and their bare backs gleamed in the rising sun like row after row of company houses in the early morning.

"It's on!" somebody cried. "The power is on!"

"Will has turned on the power," Griselda said, dancing with joy. She was on the verge of bursting into tears again. "Will did it! It was Will! Will turned the power on!"

All of them were too excited to speak coherently. They jumped up and down on their toes, each trying to see over the head of the other. Men ran to the windows shaking their fists into the air. Some of them were laughing, some were cursing, some were standing as though they were in a daze. When the machinery turned, they ran back and stood in their accustomed positions beside the looms.

There was a sound of sudden small explosions in the eastern end of the mill. It sounded like small firecrackers bursting. In the roar of the machinery it had almost been drowned out, but it was loud enough to be heard.

Everyone turned his head to look down at the eastern end of the mill. Down there the power room was located.

"What was that?" Griselda asked, clutching Rosamond.

Rosamond was like a ghost. Her face was drawn and white, and her pale lips were dry like cotton.

The other women began talking excitedly among themselves. They spoke in whispers, in hushed undertones that made no sound.

"Rosamond, what was that?" Griselda cried frantically. "Rosamond, answer me!"

"I don't know," she murmured.

Darling Jill trembled beside her sister. She could feel a convulsive throb serge through her heart and head. She leaned heavily upon Griselda for support.

A man on one of the middle floors ran to a window and shook his fist into the air, cursing and shouting. They could see warm blood trickle from the corners of his lips, dropping to his bare chest. He raised his fists into the air, screaming to the heavens.

Soon others ran to the windows excitedly, staring down into the crowd of wives and sisters below, cursing and shouting while their fists shook the air.

"What's the matter?" a woman in the crowd cried. "What happened? Dear God, help us!"

The windows were filled with cursing, bare-chested men who looked down into the faces of the women and girls.

Suddenly there was a cessation of noise in the mill. The machinery whirled to a stop, dying. There was not a sound anywhere, not even in the crowd below. Women turned to each other, helplessly.

First one man, his bare chest gleaming in the sun, appeared at the big double-doors below. He came out slowly, his hands holding fists that were too weak to remain doubled any longer. Another man came behind him, then two, then others. The door was filled with men walking slowly, turning at the steps until the glow of the sun covered their pale backs with thin blood.

"What happened?" a woman cried. "Tell us what happened! What's wrong?"

Rosamond and Darling Jill and Griselda were not close enough to hear what the men answered in weak voices. They stood on tiptoes, clutching each other, waiting to see Will and to hear from him what the trouble was.

A woman nearby screamed, sending shudders through Griselda. She cried with the pain of the woman's scream.

They pushed and fought their way towards the men coming from the Mill. Griselda clung to Rosamond, Darling Jill clung to Griselda. They went forward slowly, pushing frantically through the crowd to the men coming so slowly from the mill.

"Where's Will?" Griselda cried.

A man turned and looked at them. He came toward them to speak to the three of them.

"You're Will Thompson's wife, aren't you?"

"Where is Will?" Rosamond cried, throwing herself upon the man's bare chest.

"They shot him."

"Who shot him?"

"Will! Will! Will!"

"Those Piedmont guards shot him."

"Dear God!"

"Is he badly hurt?"

"He's dead."

That was all. There was no more to hear.

The women and girls behind them were silent like people in slumber. They pressed forward, supporting Will Thompson's widow and sisters-in-law.

More men filed out, walking slowly up the hill towards the long rows of yellow company houses, while the muscles on their bare backs hung like cut tendons under the skin. There was a man with blood on his lips. He spat into the yellow dust at his feet. Another man coughed, and blood oozed through the corners of his tightly compressed mouth. He spat into the yellow dust of Carolina.

Women were beginning to leave, running to the sides of the men and walking beside them up the hill towards the long rows of yellow company houses. There were tears in the eyes of the girls so beautiful who walked homeward with their lovers. These were the girls of the Valley whose breasts were erect and whose faces were like morning-glories when they stood in the windows of the ivy-walled mill.

Rosamond was not beside Griselda and Darling Jill when they turned to put their arms around her. She had run towards the mill door. She fell against the side of the building, clutching in her hands the ivy that grew so beautifully.

They ran to be with her.

"Will!" Rosamond cried frantically. "Will! Will!"

They put their arms around her and held her.

Several men stepped out the door and waited. Then several others came out slowly, carrying the body of Will Thompson. They tried to keep his wife and sisters-in-law back, but they ran closer until they could look at him.

"Oh, he's dead!" Rosamond said.

She had not realized that Will was dead until she saw his limp body. She still could not believe that he would not come to life. She could not believe that he would never be alive again.

The men in front took Rosamond and Darling Jill and Griselda up the hill towards the long rows of yellow company houses, holding them and supporting them. The bare backs of the men were strong with their arms around Will Thompson's wife and sisters-in-law.

When they reached the front of the house, the body was kept in the street until a place could be provided for it. The three women were carried to the house. Women from the yellow company houses up the street and down it came running to help.

"I don't know what we're going to do now," a man said. "Will Thompson isn't here any more."

Another man looked down at the ivy-walled mill.

"They were afraid of Will," he said. "They knew he had the guts to fight back. I don't reckon there'll be any use of trying to fight them without Will. They'll try to run now and make us take a dollar-ten. If Will Thompson was here, we wouldn't do it. Will Thompson would fight them."

The body was carried to the porch and placed in the shade of the room. His back was bare, but the three drying blood-clogged holes were hidden from sight.

"Let's turn him over," somebody said. "Everybody ought to know how Will Thompson was shot in the back by those sons-of-bitches down there."

"We'll bury him tomorrow. And I reckon everybody in Scottsville will be at the funeral. Everybody but those sons-of-bitches down there."

"What's his wife going to do now? She's all alone."

"We'll take care of her, if she'll let us. She's Will Thompson's widow."

An ambulance came up the street and the strong bare-backed men lifted the body from the porch and carried it out to the street. The three women in the house came to the door and stood close together while the bare-backed men carried Will from the porch and put him into the ambulance. He was Will Thompson now. He belonged to those bare-backed men with bloody lips. He belonged to Horse Creek Valley now. He was not theirs any longer. He was Will Thompson.

The three women stood in the door watching the rear end of the ambulance while it went slowly down the street to the undertaker. The body would be prepared for burial, and the next day there would be a funeral in the cemetery on the hill that looked down upon Horse Creek Valley. The men with blood-stained lips who carried him down to his grave would some day go back to the mill to card and spin and weave and dye. Will Thompson would breathe no more lint into his lungs.

Inside the house one of the men was trying to explain to Pluto how Will had been killed. Pluto was more frightened than ever. Until that time he had been scared of only the darkness in Scottsville, but now he was afraid of the day also. Men were killed in broad daylight in the Valley. He wished he could make Darling Jill and Griselda go home right away. If he had to remain in the yellow company house another night, he knew he probably would not sleep. The man with the bare chest and back sat in the room with Pluto, talking to him about the mill, but Pluto was not listening any longer. He had become afraid of the man beside him; he was afraid the man would suddenly turn with a knife in his hand and cut his throat from ear to ear. He knew then that he was out of place in a cotton mill town. The country, back at home in Marion, was the place for him to go as quickly as possible. He promised himself he would never again leave it if only he could get back safely this time.

Late that evening some of the women from the yellow company houses on the street came and prepared the first meal any of them had had that day. Will had eaten breakfast early that morning, but none of the others had. Pluto felt starved after missing two meals. He had never been so hungry in all his life. Back home in Marion he had never been forced to go hungry for the lack of food. He could smell the cooking food and the boiling coffee through the open doors, and he was unable to sit still. He got up and went to the door just as one of the women came to call him to the kitchen. Out in

the hall he became frightened again and would have gone
back, but the woman took his arm and went with him to the
kitchen.

While he was there, Darling Jill came in and sat down
beside him. He felt much safer then. Somehow, he felt that
she was a protection in a foreign country. She ate a little, and
when she had finished, she remained seated beside him.

Later, Pluto ventured to ask Darling Jill when they could
go back to Georgia.

"Tomorrow as soon as the funeral is over," she said.

"Can't we go now?"

"Of course not."

"They can bury Will all right without us," he suggested.
"They'll do it all right. I wish I could go home right away,
Darling Jill. I don't feel safe in Scottsville."

"Hush, Pluto. Don't be such a child."

He remained silent after that. Darling Jill took his hand
and led him to one of the dark rooms across the hall. He felt
exactly as he once had many years before when he was a
small boy holding the hand of his mother in a dark night.

Outside the windows was the sound of the Valley town
with all its strange noises and unfamiliar voices. He was glad
the street light shone through the leaves of the tree and partly
lighted the room. It was safer with a little light, and he was not
so afraid as he had been earlier that evening. If somebody
should come to the window and crawl inside to slit his throat
from ear to ear he would be able to see them before he felt
the blade under his chin.

Darling Jill had brought him to the bed and had made
him lie down upon it. He was reluctant to release her hand,
and when he saw that she was going to lie down beside him,
he was no longer afraid. The Valley was still there, and the
strange company town, but he had Darling Jill to lie beside
him, her hand in his, and he could close his eyes without
fear.

Just before both of them dropped off to sleep, he felt her
arms around his neck. He turned to her, holding her tightly.
There was nothing to be afraid of then.

Chapter XVIII

TY TY WAS WAITING for them on the front porch when they reached home late that afternoon. He got up when he recognized Pluto's car, and walked across the yard to meet them before the automobile was brought to a stop.

"Where in the pluperfect hell have you folks been the past two days, anyhow?" he demanded severely. "Me and the boys are near about starved for woman's cooking. We've been eating, yes, but a man can't get the proper nourishment out of just eating. We crave woman's cooking to satisfy us. You folks have been aggravating me like all get-out."

Pluto was ready to explain why they had not come back sooner, but Darling Jill made him be quiet.

"Where's Will Thompson?" Ty Ty asked. "Did you bring that good-for-nothing Will Thompson back again? I don't see him in the car, though."

"Hush, Pa," Griselda said, starting to cry.

"Of all the fool women, I never heard the like. Why can't I ask about Will? I only asked one question, and all of you girls started to cry. I'll be dog-gone if I ever seen the like of it."

"Will isn't here any more," Griselda said.

"What the pluperfect hell do you take me to be, anyhow? Don't you reckon I can see he ain't here?"

"Will was shot yesterday morning."

"Shot? What with—corn?"

"Killed with a pistol, Pa," Darling Jill said. "We buried Will this afternoon in the Valley. He's dead now, and covered with earth."

Ty Ty was speechless for a moment. He leaned against the car, searching each face before him. When he saw Rosamond's face, he knew it was true.

"Now, you don't mean Will Thompson," Ty Ty said. "Not our Will! Say it ain't so!"

"It is so, Pa. Will is dead now, and covered with earth over there in Horse Creek Valley."

"Trouble at the mill then, I'll bet a pretty. Or else over a female."

Rosamond got out and ran to the house. The others got out slowly and looked strangely at the buildings in the twi-

135

light. Pluto did not know whether to remain where he was or whether to go home immediately.

Ty Ty sent Darling Jill into the house to cook supper without loss of time.

"You stay here and tell me what happened to Will Thompson," he told Griselda. "I can't let our Will pass on without knowing all about it. Will was one of the family."

They left Pluto sitting on the runningboard of his car, and walked across the yard to the front steps. Ty Ty sat down and waited to hear what Griselda had to tell him about Will. She was still crying a little.

"Did they shoot him for breaking into company property, Griselda?"

"Yes, Pa. All the men in Scottsville went into the mill and tried to start it. Will was the one who turned the power on."

"Oh, so that's what he was always talking about when he said he was going to turn the power on? Well, I never did fully understand what he had in mind when he said that. And our Will turned the power on!"

"Some company police from the Piedmont shot him when he turned it on."

Ty Ty was silent for several moments. He gazed out through the gray dusk, seeing through it to the boundaries of his land. He could see each mound of earth that had been excavated, each deep round hole they had dug. And far beyond them all he could see the cleared field beyond the woods where God's little acre lay. For some reason he wished then to bring it closer to the house where he might be near it all the time. He felt guilty of something—maybe it was sacrilege or desecration —whatever it was, he knew he had not played fair with God. Now he wished to bring God's little acre back to its rightful place beside the house where he could see it all the time. He had very little in the world to live for anyway, and when men died, he could find consolation only in his love of God. He brought God's little acre back from the far side of the farm and placed it under him. He promised himself to keep it there until he died.

Ty Ty had no eulogy for Will Thompson. Will would never help them dig for gold. He laughed at them when Ty Ty asked him for help. He said it was foolish to try to find gold where there was no gold. Ty Ty knew there was gold in the ground, and he had always been a little angry with Will for laughing at his efforts to find it. Will had always seemed to be more interested in getting back to Horse Creek Valley than he was in staying there and helping Ty Ty.

"Sometimes I wished Will would stay here and help us, and sometimes I was glad he didn't. He was a fool about cotton mills, I reckon, and couldn't pretend to be a farmer. Maybe God made two kinds of us, after all. It looks like now, though I used to never think so, that God made a man to work the ground and a man to work the machinery. I reckon I was a fool to try to make Will Thompson take an interest in the land. He was always saying something about spinning and weaving, and about how pretty the girls and how hungry the men were in the Valley. I couldn't always make out what he was talking about, but sometimes I could just about feel something inside that told me all the things he said were true. He used to sit here and tell me how strong men were in the Valley when they were young and how weak they were when they grew up breathing cotton lint into their lungs and dying with blood on their lips. And Will used to say how pretty the girls were when they were young and how ugly they were when they were old and starving with pellagra. But he didn't like the land, anyway. He was one of the people of Horse Creek Valley."

Griselda pushed her hand into his. He held her hand awkwardly, not knowing why she wished him to touch her.

"You and Will were not different in every way," she said softly.

"Which way is that? It looks to me like I just finished telling you how different we were. Will was a mill man, and I'm a man of the land."

"You and Will were the only two men I've ever known who treated me as I liked to be treated."

"Now, now, Griselda. You're just all wrought up over seeing Will get shot over there in the Valley. Don't take on so about him. Everybody dies in this world sooner or later, and Will died sooner. That's all the difference."

"You and Will were real men, Pa."

"Now what in the pluperfect hell do you mean by that? I can't make heads or tails of it."

Griselda stopped crying until she could tell Ty Ty. She pushed her hands tighter into his, laying her head on his shoulder.

"You remember what you said about me sometimes—you used to say that and I'd try to make you stop—and you never would stop—that's what I mean."

"Now, I don't know. Maybe I do."

"Of course you know—those things about what a man would want to do when he saw me."

"I reckon I do. Maybe I do know what you mean."

"You and Will were the only two men who ever said that to me, Pa. All the other men I've known were too—I don't know what to say—they didn't seem to be men enough to have that feeling—they were just like all the rest. But you and Will weren't like that."

"I reckon I know what you mean."

"A woman can never really love a man unless he's like that. There's something about it that makes everything so different—it's not just liking to be kissed and things like that— most men think that's all. And Will—he said he wanted to do that—just like you did. And he wasn't afraid, either. Other men seem to be afraid to say things like that, or else they aren't men enough to want to do them. Will—Will took my clothes off and tore them to pieces and said he was going to do that. And he did, Pa. I didn't know I wanted him to do it before, but after that I was certain. After a woman has that done to her once, Pa, she's never the same again. It opens her up, or something. I could never really love another man unless he did that to me. I suppose if Will had not been killed, I would have stayed over there. I couldn't have left him after that. I would have been like a dog that loves you and follows you around no matter how mean you are to him. I would have stayed with Will the rest of my life. Because when a man does that to a woman, Pa, it makes love so strong nothing in the world can stop it. It must be God in people to do that. It's something, anyway. I have it now."

Ty Ty patted her hand. He could think of nothing to say, because there beside him sat a woman who knew as he did a secret of living. After a while he breathed deeply and lifted her head from his shoulder.

"Just try to get along with Buck somehow, Griselda. Maybe Buck will be like that when he grows older. He's not as old as Will was, and he hasn't had time to learn the things he should. Help him along as much as you can. He's my boy, and I want him to keep you. There's not another girl in ten thousand like you. If you left him, he'd never find another wife as fine as you are."

"He'll never learn, Pa. Buck just isn't like you and Will. A man has to be born that way at the start."

Ty Ty got up. "It's a pity all folks ain't got the sense dogs are born with."

Griselda put her hand on his arm and got to her feet. She stood beside him unsteadily for several moments, trying to balance herself.

"The trouble with people is that they try to fool themselves into believing that they're different from the way God made them. You go to church and a preacher tells you things that deep down in your heart you know ain't so. But most people are so dead inside that they believe it and try to make everybody else live that way. People ought to live like God made us to live. When you sit down by yourself and feel what's in you, that's the real way to live. It's feeling. Some people talk about your head being the thing to go by, but it ain't so. Your head gives you sense to show you how to deal with people when it comes to striking a bargain and things like that, but it can't feel for you. People have got to feel for themselves as God made them to feel. It's folks who let their head run them who make all the mess of living. Your head can't make you love a man, if you don't feel like loving him. It's got to be a feeling down inside of you like you and Will had."

He walked to the edge of the porch and looked up at the stars. She waited beside him until he was ready to leave.

"We'd better go in and see how supper is cooking," he told her.

They walked through the dark hall, smelling the aroma of freshly ground coffee. Nearer the kitchen they could smell frying ham on the stove.

Buck looked up at Griselda from his chair behind the partly opened door when they walked into the brightly lighted kitchen where the others were. She had to turn her head and shoulders halfway around in order to see him. He glared at her surlily.

"I reckon if he hadn't been shot, you'd still be over there, wouldn't you?"

The words were on the tip of her tongue to shout at him that she would, but she bit her lips and tried to keep from speaking just then.

"You and him got pretty thick, didn't you?"

"Please, Buck," she begged.

"Please, what? Don't want me to talk about it, huh?"

"There's nothing to talk about. And anyway, you ought to have some regard for Rosamond."

He looked at Rosamond. She stood with her back to him turning the ham in the griddles.

"What's wrong with me? Why did you have to chase off

after him? Don't you think I'm good enough for you, huh?"

"Please, Buck, not now."

"If you were going to run around with your legs spread open, why in hell didn't you take better aim? That son-of-a-bitch was a lint-head. A lint-head from Horse Creek Valley!"

"There's no particular spot in the world where real men live," Darling Jill said. "You can find just as many in Horse Creek Valley as you can on The Hill in Augusta, or on farms around Marion."

Buck turned and looked her up and down.

"You talk like you've been pricked, too. What in hell went on over there, anyhow?"

Ty Ty thought it was time to step in before things went too far. He laid his hand on Buck's shoulder and tried to quiet him. Buck threw his father's hand off, moving his chair to another part of the kitchen.

"Now, son," he said, "don't go and get all heated up over nothing."

"To hell with that talk," he shouted. "You stay out of this and stop trying to take up for her."

The girls began carrying the supper dishes into the next room and placing them on the wide table. They all went into the dining-room and sat down. Buck had not said all he wished to say, by any means. He merely transferred the scene from one room to the other.

"Go get Pluto, Darling Jill," Ty Ty said. "He'll sit out there in the yard all night and not get a bite to eat if somebody doesn't look out for him."

Griselda sat with lowered head, her eyes averted. She hoped Buck would not say anything else while Rosamond was in the room. It hurt her to have Buck talk about Will in Rosamond's presence, and so soon after the funeral, too.

Pluto came back with Darling Jill and took his accustomed seat at the table. He could feel the tension in the room, and he took care to keep his mouth shut unless he was spoken to. He was afraid that Buck was going to ask him what had happened in Scottsville.

After several minutes of silence, Ty Ty tried to take advantage of it to change the subject.

"A man was out here watching us dig yesterday, and he tried to tell me I called the lode by the wrong name. He said he used to mine gold up in North Georgia, and up there a lode was a streak of gold in the rock. He said what we were aiming at was placering. I told him as long as we struck gold, I didn't give a dog-gone what name he called it by."

"He was right," Shaw said. "In high school the teachers said placer mining was getting gold out of dirt or gravel. Lode mining is by blasting it out of rock and crushing it and cooking it out with heat."

"Well, he still may be right, and you too, son," Ty Ty said, shaking his head, "but a load of gold is what I've got my heart set on. That will be my ship coming in, and I don't give a dog-gone for the name you call it. You can call it lode mining or placer mining, whichever you want, but when I get a load of it, I'll know dog-gone well my ship has come in."

"The man said the only way nuggets could get into the ground around here would be by a flood washing them down a long time ago, and then being covered up with silt."

"The man you mention don't know no more about digging for gold on my land than one of those mules out there. I've been doing it for nearly fifteen years, and I reckon if anybody knows what I'm doing, I do. Let the man have his say, but don't pay him no heed, son. Too many men talking will get you all balled up, and you won't know which way is straight up and which is straight down."

Buck leaned over the table.

"I reckon if I was to put my hands on you now, you'd say, 'Ouch! Don't do that, Buck. I'm sore there.'" He looked at Griselda steadily. "Can't you talk? What's the matter with you?"

"Of course, I can talk, Buck," she pleaded. "Please don't say such things now."

Pluto looked at Darling Jill uneasily. He dreaded for the time to come when Buck would ask him what had happened in Scottsville.

"Well, he's dead now," Buck said, "and I can't do much about it, to him. But if he wasn't, I'd sure do something you wouldn't forget. I'd take that gun hanging up there and do plenty. It's a God damn shame you can't kill a man but once. I'd like to kill him just as long as I could buy shells to fire at him."

Rosamond cried. She laid down her knife and fork and ran from the room.

"Now, see what you've done!" Darling Jill said. "You ought to be ashamed of yourself for doing a thing like that."

"You and her," he said, pointing his fork at Griselda, "you and her don't look ashamed for anything. If I was married to you, I'd choke hell out of you. You're as loose as a busted belly-band on a gray mule."

"Now, son," Ty Ty said. "She's your sister."

"What of it? She's loose, ain't she, sister or no sister? I'd choke hell out of her if she was my wife."

"If you're not man enough to hold your wife, you ought to be too ashamed to say anything," Darling Jill told him. "You ought to go somewhere and hide your face."

"We're going on like this all the time," Ty Ty said wearily, "and we're getting further and further away from the happy life. All of us ought to sit down and think a little about living, and how to do it. God didn't put us here to scrap and fight each other all the time. If we don't have a little more love for each other, one of these days there's going to be deep sorrow in my heart. I've tried all my life to keep a peaceful family under my roof. I've got my head set on having just that all my days, and I don't aim to give up trying now. You folks see if you can't stop your scrapping and laugh just a little, and I'll feel much better. That's the finest cure in the world for scrapping and fighting."

"You talk like a damn fool," Buck said disgustedly.

"Maybe it does sound that way to you, Buck. But when you get God in your heart, you have a feeling that living is worth striving for night and day. I ain't talking about the God you hear about in the churches, I'm talking about the God inside of a body. I've got the greatest feeling for Him, because He helps me to live. That's why I set aside God's little acre out there on the farm when I was just a young man starting in. I like to have something around me that I can go to and stand on and feel God in."

"He ain't got a penny out of it yet," Shaw said, laughing a little.

"You boys don't seem to catch on, son. It ain't so important that I get money out of God's little acre to give to the church and the preacher, it's just the fact that I set that up in His name. All you boys seem to think about is the things you can see and touch—that ain't living. It's the things you can feel inside of you—that's what living is made for. True, as you say, God ain't got a penny of money out of that piece of ground, but it's the fact that I set God's little acre aside out there that matters. That's the sign that God's in my heart. He knows I ain't striking it rich down here, but He ain't interested in how much money a man makes. What tickles Him is the fact that I set aside a part of my land for Him just to show that I have got some of Him inside of me."

"Why don't you go to church more than you do then?" Shaw asked. "If you believe so much in God, why don't you go there oftener?"

"That ain't a fair question, son. You know good and well how tired I am when Sunday comes, after digging all week long in the holes. God doesn't miss me there, anyhow. He knows why I can't come. I've spoken to Him about such things all my life, and He knows pretty well all about it."

"What's all that got to do with her?" Buck asked, pointing his fork at Griselda. "I was talking about her before you butted in about something else."

"Nothing, son. I ain't got a thing in the world to do with her. She already knows about it. I was talking for your benefit so you would try to learn more about living. If I was you, son, when I went to bed tonight, I'd get down on my knees in the dark and talk to God about it. He can tell you things nobody else can, and maybe He'll tell you how you ought to act with Griselda. He'll tell you, if you'll only take the time and trouble to listen, because if there's anything in the world He's crazy about, it's seeing a man and a woman fools about each other. He knows then that the world is running along as slick as grease."

Chapter XIX

Ty Ty stayed up late that night trying to talk to Buck. He knew it was a duty he owed his children to convince them that living was deeper than the surface they saw. The girls seemed to realize that, but the boys did not. Ty Ty knew there would be plenty of time later to talk to Shaw, and he gave all his attention to Buck for Griselda's sake. Buck was irritated by the things he tried to explain and he acted as though he did not wish to understand.

"You boys just don't seem to catch on," Ty Ty said, dropping his hands at his sides. "You boys seem to think that if you have a little money to spend and a new raincoat or some such knickknack and a belly full of barbecue, there ain't another thing to be concerned about. I wish I could tell you all about it. It's a ticklish thing to try to explain, because I don't know none too much about using words, and if I did know, it wouldn't help matters much because it's something you've got to feel. It's just like the fellow said: 'It's there, or it ain't there, and there are only two ways about it.' You boys appear like it ain't there. Just take a walk off by yourself some time and think about it, and maybe it will come to you. I don't know what else to tell you to do."

"I don't know what in hell you're trying to say," Buck
broke in, "but if it's what Griselda's got, I don't want it.
She went over there to Horse Creek Valley and got shot full
of something. And if you ask me, I'll say it was some of Will
Thompson. That lint-head!"

"Will Thompson was a real man," Darling Jill said.

"A real man, huh? And you got a shot, too, didn't you?
It's a damn good sign when you come back here with your
mind made up to marry Pluto Swint all of a sudden. You'd
be in a mess now if he wouldn't marry you."

"Will was a real man, anyway."

"What in hell is a real man? Will Thompson wasn't any
bigger than I am. He wasn't any stronger, either. I could throw
him any morning before breakfast."

"It wasn't the way he looked that made him different.
It was how he was made inside. He could feel things, and
you can't."

Buck got up and looked at them for a moment from the
door.

"What do you take me for, anyway—a sucker? Don't
you reckon I know damn well you and Griselda are making
up that for an excuse? I'm not all that dumb. You can't suck
me in with that kind of talk."

He left the house and no one knew where he had gone.
Ty Ty waited a while, thinking Buck might come back in
a few minutes and listen with more reason after he had
cooled off in the night, but at twelve he had not returned.
Ty Ty got up then to go to bed.

"Buck will come around all right when he gets a little
older, Griselda. Just try to be patient with him till he lives
a little more. It takes some people a lifetime, almost, to learn
some things."

"I'm afraid he'll never learn," she said. "Not before it's
too late, anyway."

Ty Ty patted her shoulder.

"You girls are all wrought up over Will getting killed.
Just go to bed now and get a good night's sleep. Tomorrow
morning things will look a lot different."

"But he's dead," Darling Jill said. "I can't forget that
he's dead."

"Maybe it's best that he is now. The three of you couldn't
have stayed over there in Scottsville. Rosamond was married
to him, and you and Griselda would have made a mess that
the law doesn't allow."

Long after everybody else in the house was asleep, Ty

Ty lay awake thinking. Buck had not returned, and Griselda was alone in the room across the hall, crying. For nearly an hour he had lain on his side listening to the restless toss of her body as she lay sleepless upon the bed. But she finally became quiet, and he knew she had fallen to sleep at last. Ty Ty wondered where Buck had gone. There was no need for him to get up and go out in the night looking for him, so he tried to dismiss Buck from his thoughts.

Some time in the night he heard Darling Jill go to the back porch for a drink of water. He could hear her walking in her soft-soled slippers through the hall past his door. She remained on the porch only a minute and came back into the house. Ty Ty turned over and looked through the door into the dark hall when he heard her returning. He could see dimly the moving light of her nightgown, and he could have reached out and touched her with the tips of his fingers when she passed the door. He was about to ask her if she were ill, but he thought better of it. He knew she was not sick, anyway; there was nothing the matter with her except that which also made Rosamond and Griselda restless. He allowed her to go back to her bed without speaking. All three of them would feel much better after several hours of sleep. When breakfast was over, he would try to say something to them.

At daybreak Buck still had not returned to the house. Ty Ty lay a little while staring at the beginning of light on the ceiling, turning later to watch the gray dawn break into day. When he heard Black Sam and Uncle Felix talking in an undertone in the yard, he jumped out of bed and dressed quickly. He looked out the window and saw the two colored men sitting on the rim of the crater, their feet hanging over the side, waiting for him to start them to work.

He left the room and walked out into the yard.

"Did you see Buck anywhere?" he asked Uncle Felix.

Uncle Felix shook his head.

"Mr. Buck didn't get up this early already, did he?" Black Sam asked.

"He stayed out somewhere all night. I reckon he'll show up before long."

"Trouble in your house, boss?" Uncle Felix asked cautiously.

"Trouble?" Ty Ty repeated. "Who said there was trouble in the house?"

"When white folks don't stay in the house to sleep, there's pretty nearly always trouble."

Ty Ty sat down several feet away, looking down into the big hole at his right. He knew it was useless to try to lie to Negroes. They always knew.

"Maybe there was trouble," he said. "It's about over with now, though. One of them got killed, and I don't look for much after today. It's all over with now, I hope."

"Who got killed?" Black Sam asked. "I didn't hear about anybody getting killed, Mr. Ty Ty. That's news to me."

"It was Will Thompson, over there in Horse Creek Valley. Somebody shot him over there day before yesterday. The girls got all excited about it, and I've had a hard time trying to calm them down."

"I sure reckon you do have a hard time trying to do that, boss. It's pretty hard to calm the women folks down after the male man's gone."

Ty Ty turned around quickly, looking at Black Sam.

"What in the pluperfect hell are you talking about, anyhow?"

"Nothing, Mr. Ty Ty. Nothing at all."

"Go on to work," he said shortly. "The sun's been up half an hour already. We can't get nothing done if we're going to wait till after the sun rises before we start digging. The only way to strike that lode, I've been thinking, is to dig and dig and dig."

The two colored men went down into the ground. Black Sam was singing a little, but Uncle Felix was waiting for Ty Ty to leave so he could talk to Black Sam about the trouble in the house. Presently he looked up to the top where Ty Ty had been standing. Ty Ty had gone from sight.

"That Buck would have killed him pretty soon himself," Uncle Felix said. "He would have done it first if he hadn't been so slow to catch on. I saw that look in his wife's eyes a long long time ago when Will Thompson first started coming over here to Georgia. She was getting ready to make way for him then. It didn't look to me like she knew it herself, but I could see it a mile off. That other girl was getting ready for the same thing, too. They just had to make way for Mr. Will. Wasn't no stopping them."

"Who you mean?"

"Darling Jill's the other one I mean."

"Man, man! black fellow, that wasn't nothing new for her. That white girl's always been like that. I've stopped paying any attention to her. But I reckon she was getting ready for it a heap sooner than she generally does, because

Mr. Will just naturally made them all that way. But that Griselda is the one to watch. She makes a man itch all over till he don't know where to scratch first."

"Lord, Lord!"

"I was born unlucky. I wish I was a white man myself. She's got what I'm talking about."

"Lord, Lord!"

"One day I was passing the window around yonder and I looked in."

"What did you see, nigger? The moon rising?"

"What I saw made me just want to get right straight away down on my hands and knees and lick something."

"Lord, Lord!"

"I was born unlucky."

"Ain't it the truth!"

"Trouble in the house."

"Lord, Lord!"

"One man's dead."

"And trouble in the house."

"The male man's gone."

"He can't prick them no more."

"Lord, Lord!"

"Trouble in the house."

"My mammy was a darky——"

"My daddy was too——"

"That white gal's frisky——"

"Good Lord, what to do——"

"Lord, Lord!"

"The time ain't long."

"Somebody shot the male man."

"He can't prick them no more."

"And trouble in the house."

"Lord, Lord!"

Ty Ty shouted down into the hole from the ground above. They picked the clay without looking up. Ty Ty slid down into the crater, bringing a yard of loose sand and clay with him.

"Buck's come back, and I don't want you to say anything to him about staying out all night. I've got enough trouble on my hands, Uncle Felix, without making more. Just leave him alone and don't ask him where he's been. I've got all the trouble now I can stand."

They nodded while he looked at them.

"Somebody shot the male man," Black Sam said aloud.

Ty Ty wheeled around.

"What did you say?"

"Yes, sir, boss. Yes, sir. We won't say nothing to him."

He started up the side of the hole.

"He can't prick them no more."

Ty Ty stopped. Suddenly he jumped from the side of the crater, turning around in the air.

"What in the pluperfect hell are you darkies saying?"

"Yes, sir, boss. Yes, sir. We won't say nothing to Mr. Buck. We won't say nothing at all."

Once more he started climbing to the top.

"Trouble in the house," Black Sam said aloud.

Ty Ty stopped for the third time, but he did not turn around. He waited there, listening.

"Yes, sir, boss. Yes, sir. We won't say nothing to Mr. Buck. We won't say nothing at all."

He'll be down here in a little while, and I want him left alone. If I hear you talking to him about staying out all night, I'll come down in here with a singletree and knock your blocks clear off your shoulders."

"Yes, sir, boss," Black Sam said, "Yes, sir, whiteboss. We ain't saying nothing to Mr. Buck."

Ty Ty climbed up the side of the hole, leaving the colored men silent. He was confident that they would obey his orders. They were smart Negroes.

Up on the ground Ty Ty met Buck coming to work. He put his arm around his son's shoulder when they met. Neither of them said anything, and after a moment Buck turned from Ty Ty and slid down into the crater with the two colored men. Ty Ty stood above for several minutes watching them shovel the clay. Later he left and walked around to the front yard.

Coming down the road from the Marion-Augusta highway was a big car blowing up a cloud of dust. At first Ty Ty thought it was Pluto, but the car was traveling twice as fast as Pluto ever dared drive, and, besides that, it was a larger car and it was shiny black with nickeled trimming that glistened in the sun like new half-dollars.

"Now, who can that be?" Ty Ty asked himself, stopping at the water-oak to watch its approach.

The automobile was at the yard before he realized it. The driver slowed down in a quickly enveloping cloud of yellow dust, coming to a stop so suddenly that the dust passed on in front of it.

Ty Ty ran several steps toward the large black car. It

came into the yard then, swaying on the deep springs and roaring in its long motor.

With mouth agape he saw Jim Leslie step out and come towards him. He could not imagine seeing Jim Leslie there. It was the first time in nearly fifteen years that he had set foot on the place.

"Well, I'll declare!" Ty Ty said, running forward to grasp his son's hand.

"Glad to see you, Pa," Jim Leslie said. "Where's Griselda?"

"Who?"

"Griselda."

"You didn't come out here to ask that, did you, son?"

"Where is she?"

"You must be all balled up, Jim Leslie. Didn't you come to see the whole family?"

Jim Leslie started towards the house. Ty Ty ran and caught up with him, pulling his arm and stopping him quickly.

"Now, wait a minute, son. Just hold your horses. What do you want to see Buck's wife about?"

"I haven't got time to talk to you now. I'm in a big hurry. Turn my arm loose."

"Now, listen, son," Ty Ty begged, "there's sorrow here in the house now."

"What about it? What's the matter?"

"Will Thompson was killed the other day over in Scottsville. The girls in the house are nervous and sad. I don't want you to come here and make a mess. You come on out to the hole and sit and talk to the boys and me. When you get tired of staying, then just turn around and go on back to Augusta. We'll all take a trip up there next week to see you when the girls have calmed down some."

"There's nothing the matter with Griselda. What's she got to do with Will Thompson getting killed? He wasn't anything to her. She wouldn't get mixed up with a lint-head from Horse Creek Valley."

"Now, son, I know a heap more right now than you do, and I ask you not to go in there. Women are queer creatures, and man don't always understand them. I can't tell you about it now, but I ask you to stay out of that house. Just get back into your car and turn around and go on back to Augusta where you came from. Now go on, son, before trouble starts."

"What's that got to do with me?" Jim Leslie asked crossly. "Will Thompson is out of this. Griselda wouldn't have anything to do with a lint-head."

"Will Thompson being a lint-head, as you call him, hasn't anything to do with it, either."

"Turn me loose, then. I'm in a big hurry. I haven't got time to stand here arguing with you. I know what I want, and I came after it."

Ty Ty saw that he was powerless to keep Jim Leslie from the house, but he was determined to do all he could to keep trouble from starting. He decided that the best thing to do was to call Buck and Shaw, and the three of them would be able to force Jim Leslie back into his car.

He called Buck, and waited, still holding Jim Leslie's arm. Jim Leslie looked all around, expecting to see Buck suddenly appear at any moment.

"It won't do any good to call him, because I'm not scared of him. Where is he, anyway?"

"He's down in the hole digging."

Ty Ty called again, listening for Buck's answer.

"Still digging for gold," Jim Leslie laughed. "And even Buck and Shaw. It looks like you and the rest of them would have learned your lesson by now. You ought to go to work raising something on this land. Raising piles of dirt is the nearest you've come to it yet."

"I aim to strike the lode soon."

"That's the same thing you said fourteen or fifteen years ago. Age didn't bring you any sense."

"I've got sense you don't know about, son."

Buck came around the corner of the house. He was surprised to see Jim Leslie there, but he came forward to find out why he had been called. Several feet away he stopped and looked at his older brother suspiciously.

"What do you want?" he asked.

"I didn't call you," Jim Leslie said. "Ask him. He was the one who called."

Ty Ty turned to Jim Leslie.

"Now, son, I ask you once more to get in your car and go on back to Augusta before trouble starts. You know I can't stop Buck once he gets started, and I don't want no trouble here on the place."

Ty Ty waited a moment, hoping that Jim Leslie would do as he had been asked. He made no reply to his father. Even the appearance of Buck did not deter him from his announced intentions.

"Now, son," Ty Ty said, "Jim Leslie is here. We don't want to have no trouble. He's as welcome as the day is long.

But if he starts in the house, well—he just ain't going in there, that's all."

Jim Leslie turned his back on them and started up the porch steps. He was halfway up when he felt his arm being twisted in its socket.

"No, you don't," Buck said, releasing him. "You stay in the yard, or you leave."

Ty Ty yelled for Shaw to come running.

Chapter XX

"Now, son," Ty Ty said to Buck, "Jim Leslie has come out here and I want him to leave in a peaceful manner. I've aimed all my life to have a peaceful family, and I can't stand here and see you boys scrap. You must tell Jim Leslie, son. that we don't want no trouble out here. If he'll get in his car and turn around and go on back to Augusta, everything will be all right and like it was before he came. I wouldn't know what to think of myself if it turned out that you boys would scrap all over the place."

Ty Ty saw the two colored men at the corner of the house looking at the scene in the yard. Only their heads were showing, and their eyes were the shade of whitewash on a sunny day. When they had first heard Ty Ty calling for Buck, they knew something was about to happen up on top of the ground, and they had come up to see what the trouble was. Hearing Ty Ty order Jim Leslie into his car, they turned and walked softly out of sight around the other side of the house. After passing the rear of the building, they tiptoed towards the barn, holding their hats in their hands, and trying their best not to look back over their shoulders.

"What do you want out here?" Buck asked his brother, blocking his way on the porch.

"I didn't come out here to talk to you," Jim Leslie replied curtly.

"If you can't talk, then get to hell away from here, and be quick about it."

"Now, son," Ty Ty said.

Jim Leslie turned his back again and started up the steps to the porch. Buck still blocked the way, but Jim Leslie pushed past him.

"Now, wait a minute, you son-of-a-bitch."

"This here now scrapping has got to quit," Ty Ty shouted. "I don't aim to have it on my land."

"Wait?" Jim Leslie replied to his brother. "What for? I'm in a hurry. I can't wait."

Buck struck him on the jaw, knocking him against the side of the house. Jim Leslie crouched low over his knees and sprung at Buck.

When he saw what had happened, Ty Ty ran between them, trying his best to pry them apart. He had to duck his head every moment or two in order to keep from being hit by one of the four fists that flew all around him. He succeeded in pushing Jim Leslie against the wall, and then he tried to hold Buck.

"Now, wait a minute, boys," he said. "You boys are brothers, the three of you. You know good and well you don't want to fight each other. Every one of you wants to be peaceful, and I aim to keep you that way. Let's all just walk down to the barn and talk things over calmly and without scrapping like a pack of bobcats. I've got some things to tell you down there. There's a heap I can explain if you will only be calm while I try to talk. It's a sin and a shame for you to scrap like this. Now, come on and let's all walk down to the barn."

"I'll kill the son-of-a-bitch, now," Buck said, impatient with his father for talking so much.

"Let's not use swear-words at each other," Ty Ty begged. "I'm against so much swearing among brothers. It's all right at some times and places, but not among brothers."

Ty Ty thought that Buck appeared at that moment to be willing to listen if Jim Leslie would.

"He can't come out here—I'll kill him. I know what you're after. I'm no damn fool."

Shaw had not said anything, but he was standing beside Buck ready to help him the moment his help was needed. He would take up for Buck any time the choice was required. Ty Ty knew that he and Jim Leslie never got along very well together, anyway.

"This here now squabbling over women has got to stop on my land," Ty Ty said with sudden determination. He had at last realized how hopeless his efforts to make peace had been. "I've tried to settle this argument peacefully, but I ain't going to stand for you boys scrapping each other over women no longer. It's going to stop right now. You get in your car, son, Jim Leslie, and go on back to Augusta. Buck, you and Shaw go on back to the hole and dig. I've let this scrapping go as far as I'm going to stand for. Go on now, all of you. This here now squabbling over women has got to stop on my land."

"I'll kill the son-of-a-bitch, now." Buck said. "I'll kill him if he goes in that house, now. He can't come out here and take Griselda off, now."

"Boys, this here now squabbling over women on my land has got to stop. You all boys go on and do like I told you to do just now."

Jim Leslie saw his opportunity, and he sprang for the door and was in the house before they could stop him. Buck was only three steps behind him, however, and Ty Ty and Shaw ran after them. Jim Leslie ran through the first door he reached, and on into another room. He did not know where Griselda was, and he continued through the house in search of her.

"Stop him, Buck!" Shaw shouted. "Make him come back through the hall—don't let him get away through the back door!"

In the dining-room when Ty Ty reached it a moment later, Jim Leslie was in the middle of the room, with the table between Buck and himself, and they were cursing each other. Over in the corner the three girls were huddled behind a chair they had pulled in front of them. Griselda was crying, and so was Rosamond. Darling Jill looked as if she did not know whether to cry or to laugh. Ty Ty could not stop to look at them any longer, and he did not try to protect them so long as they were in no immediate danger, but began shouting at the boys again. He soon saw it was useless. They did not hear a word he said; they appeared to be unaware of his presence in the room.

"Come out of that corner, Griselda," Jim Leslie told her. "You're going with me. Come out of that corner and get into the car before I have to come and pull you out."

"You stay where you are and don't move," Buck told her out of the corner of his mouth, his eyes still on his brother.

Ty Ty turned to Shaw in desperation.

"You'd better go get Black Sam and Uncle Felix to help us. It looks like we can't handle him alone."

"You stay here, Shaw," Buck said. "I don't need any help. I can handle him by myself."

"Come out of that corner before I drag you out, Griselda," Jim Leslie said again.

"You came to get her, huh? Why didn't you say that in the yard? I knew damn well what it was, but I've just been waiting to hear you say it. You came to get her, huh?"

"This here now squabbling over women on my land has got to quit." Ty Ty said determinedly. "I just ain't going to stand for it no longer."

"Come out of that corner, Griselda," Jim Leslie said for the third time.

"I'll kill the son-of-a-bitch, now," Buck said.

He stepped back, relaxing his muscles.

"This here now squabbling over women on my land has got to stop," Ty Ty said, banging his fists on the table between his two sons.

Buck stepped back to the wall behind him and reached for the shotgun on the rack. He unbreeched it, looking down a moment to see if both barrels were loaded.

When Jim Leslie saw Buck with the gun, he ran out the door into the hall and on through the house to the front yard. Buck was behind him, holding out the gun in front of him as though it were a snake on a stick.

Out in the yard, Ty Ty realized it was useless for him to try to stop Buck. He could not wrestle the gun away from him; Buck was too strong. He would throw him aside without much effort. So, instead of running out into the yard, Ty Ty sank to his knees on the porch and began praying.

Behind him in the hall stood Griselda and Rosamond and Darling Jill, afraid to come any further, but scared to stay alone in the house. They huddled behind the front door, peeping through the crack to see what was happening in the yard.

Ty Ty looked up from his prayer, one eye open in fright, one eye closed in supplication, when he heard Buck shout to Jim Leslie to stop running. Jim Leslie was in front of his automobile, and he could easily have jumped behind it for protection, but instead he stopped where he was and shook his fist at Buck.

"I reckon you'll leave her alone now," Buck said.

The gun was already leveled at Jim Leslie. Ty Ty could almost see through the sights from where he was on the porch, and he was certain he could feel Buck's finger tighten on the trigger. He closed his eyes prayerfully a second before the explosion in the barrel. He opened his eyes to see Jim Leslie reach forward for something to grip for support, and heard almost immediately the explosion of the second shell. Jim Leslie stood upright for a few short seconds, and then his body twisted to one side and he fell heavily on the hard white sand under the water-oak tree.

Griselda and Rosamond and Darling Jill screamed behind the door at the same moment. Ty Ty closed his eyes again, trying to erase from his mind each horrible detail of the scene. He hoped, opening them, to find that it had all vanished. It was no different than before, however, except that Buck was standing over Jim Leslie pushing new shells into the gun. Jim Leslie twisted and doubled up into a round ball.

Ty Ty got up and ran down into the yard. He pushed Buck away and bent over Jim Leslie trying to speak to him. Without help he lifted his son in his arms and carried him to the porch. Shaw came and looked down at his brother, and the girls stood in the doorway with their hands over their faces. Every moment or so one of them would scream. Buck sat down on the steps, dropping the shotgun at his feet.

"Say you ain't going to die, son," Ty Ty begged, getting down beside him on the floor.

Jim Leslie looked up at him, closing his eyes in the glare of the sun. His lips moved for a number of seconds, but Ty Ty could not hear a sound.

"Can't we do something for him, Pa?" Rosamond asked him. She was the first to come from the hall. "What can we do, Pa?"

She knelt down with him, holding her throat with her hands. Griselda and Darling Jill came a little closer, looking down at Jim Leslie.

Ty Ty nodded to Rosamond.

"Hold his hand, Rosamond," he said. "That's what his mother would do if she was here now."

Jim Leslie opened his eyes and looked up at her when he became conscious of her hands over his.

"Can't you say something, son?" Ty Ty asked. "Just a little something, son."

"I haven't anything to say," he answered weakly, closing his eyes again.

The handkerchief in Ty Ty's hand slipped from the wound in Jim Leslie's chest and fell to the porch. Jim Leslie's eyes had opened for the last time, and they glistened in the sun, glazed and motionless.

Ty Ty got up stiffly and walked down into the yard. He walked up and down in front of the steps trying to say something to himself. He walked slowly, from one corner of the house to the other, not looking higher than the white sand he tramped upon. Griselda and Darling Jill had fallen to their knees beside Rosamond, and the three of them knelt there, breathless before the sobs came to their throats. Ty Ty did not look to see them. He knew they were there without looking.

"Blood on my land," he said. "Blood on my land."

The sound of Rosamond's running into the house behind Griselda and Darling Jill awakened him. He looked up and saw Black Sam and Uncle Felix racing across the fields towards the woods on the other side of the farm. The sight of the two colored men running away made him wonder for the first time that day where Dave was. He remembered then that he had not seen Dave since early that morning. He did not know where Dave had gone, and he did not care. He could get along somehow without him.

On the bottom step of the porch. Buck sat with his head dropped over his chest. The shotgun was still lying on the ground where it had fallen from his hands. Ty Ty turned completely around to escape the sight of it.

"Blood on my land." he muttered.

The farm before him looked desolate. The piles of red clay and yellow sand, the wide red craters between, the red soil without vegetation—the land looked desolate. In the shade of the water-oak tree where he stood, Ty Ty felt completely exhausted. He no longer felt strength in his muscles when he thought of the gold in the earth under his farm. He did not know where the gold was, and he did not know how he was going to be able to dig any longer without his strength. There was gold there though, because several nuggets had been found on the farm; he knew there was gold there, but he did not know whether he would be able to continue his search for it. At that moment he felt that there was no use in ever doing anything again. All his life he had lived with the de-termination of keeping peace in his family. Now it did not matter; nothing mattered now. Nothing mattered any longer, because blood had been spilled on his land—the blood of one of his children.

He thought himself talking to Buck in the dining-room the evening before.

"The trouble with you boys is that you don't seem to catch on."

The glare of the sun in his eyes reminded him of something else.

"Blood on my land," he repeated. "Blood on my land."

The three girls in the house were crying through the open doors and windows. While he walked up and down, they came to the porch again, standing there and looking.

"Go get an undertaker or a doctor or something, son." he told Shaw, nodding his head wearily.

Shaw got into Ty Ty's car and started to Marion. They stood on the porch watching the cloud of yellow dust left behind to settle over the roadside.

Ty Ty tried to force his eyes upon the floor so he would not lift them to look at his desolate land. He knew if he looked at it again he would feel a sinking sensation in his body. Something out there repelled him. It was no longer as it had been before. The piles of earth had always made him feel excitement; now they made him feel like turning his head away and never looking out there again. The mounds even had a different color now, and the soil of his land was nothing like earth he had ever seen before. There had never been any vegetation out there, but he had never realized the lack of it before. Over on the other side of the farm, where the newground was, there was vegetation, because the top soil in the newground had not been covered with piles of sand and clay in one place, and big yawning holes in others. He wished then that he had the strength to spread out his arms and smooth the land as far as he could see, leveling the ground by filling the holes with the mounds of earth. He realized how impotent he was by his knowledge that he would never be able to do that. He felt heavy at heart.

"Son," he said to Buck, looking off into the distance, "son, the sheriff——"

Buck raised his head for the first time and looked up into the day. He heard his father speaking to him, and he knew what had been said.

"Oh, Pa!" Rosamond screamed, standing in the door.

Ty Ty waited to hear if she would say anything else. He knew there was nothing else to say. There was no more for him to hear.

He got up and walked from one corner of the house to the other, passing in front of Buck, his lips compressed grimly, his eyes feeble.

"Son," he said, stopping at the steps, "son, the sheriff will be hearing about it when Shaw gets to town."

The girls came running down the steps to his side. Rosamond threw her arms around Buck, hugging him with all her might. Griselda was beside him crying.

"The good Lord blessed me with three of the prettiest girls a man ever had in his house. He was good to me that way, because I know I don't deserve it all."

Darling Jill had begun to cry audibly. They were all close to Ty Ty, hugging Buck in their arms.

"The good Lord blessed me that way, but He puts sorrow in my heart to pay for it. It looks like a good thing and a bad thing always have to go hand-in-hand. You don't get the one without the other, ever."

Griselda held Buck's head against her breast, stroking his hair and kissing his face. She tried to make Buck speak to her, but he closed his eyes and said nothing.

"There was a mean trick played on us somewhere. God put us in the bodies of animals and tried to make us act like people. That was the beginning of trouble. If He had made us like we are, and not called us people, the last one of us would know how to live. A man can't live, feeling himself from the inside, and listening to what the preachers say. He can't do both, but he can do one or the other. He can live like we were made to live, and feel himself on the inside, or he can live like the preachers say, and be dead on the inside. A man has got God in him from the start, and when he is made to live like a preacher says to live, there's going to be trouble. If the boys had done like I tried to get them to do, there never would have been all this trouble. The girls understand, and they are willing to live like God made them to live; but the boys go off and hear fools talk and they come back here and try to run things counter to God. God made pretty girls and He made men, and there was enough to go around. When you try to take a woman or a man and hold him off all for yourself, there ain't going to be nothing but trouble and sorrow the rest of your days."

Buck stood up, straightening his shoulders. He had one arm around Griselda, holding her while she clung to him and kissed him.

"I feel like the end of the world has struck me," Ty Ty said. "It feels like the bottom has dropped completely out from under me. I feel like I'm sinking and can't help myself."

"Don't talk like that, Pa," Darling Jill said, hugging him. "It makes me feel so bad when you say that."

Buck broke Griselda's grip around him and pushed her hands from him. She ran and threw herself upon him frantically. He could not move with her holding him.

"Son," Ty Ty said, looking out across the field piled high with earth, "son, the sheriff——"

Buck bent over and kissed Griselda full on the lips, pressing her closely for a long time. Then he pushed her away.

"Buck, where are you going?" she cried.

"I'm going for a walk," he said.

She fell upon the steps and covered her face. Darling Jill sat beside her, holding her head in her lap.

Buck went out of sight around the corner of the house, and Ty Ty followed him a moment later, walking slowly behind him. Buck climbed the fence on the other side of the well and walked in a straight line across the fields towards the newground on the other side of the farm. Ty Ty stopped at the fence and went no further. He stood there, leaning against it for support, while Buck walked slowly over the field to the newground.

He remembered then that God's little acre had been brought back to the house, and all the more acutely he realized that Jim Leslie had been killed upon it. But it was Buck that Ty Ty was thinking of at that moment, and he willed that God's little acre follow Buck, stopping when he did so that he would always be upon it. He watched Buck go towards the newground, and he was glad he had thought of God's little acre in time to have it follow Buck, stopping where Buck stopped so that his son would be upon it no matter where he went.

"Blood on my land," Ty Ty said aloud. "Blood on my land."

After a while he could no longer see Buck, and he turned towards the house and walked to the side of the big hole. The moment he looked down into the crater, he felt a consuming desire to go down to the bottom of it and dig. He went down into the hole slowly. His back was a little stiff, and his knees were weak. He was getting to be old, digging in the holes. Soon he would be too old to dig any more.

He picked up Shaw's shovel and began throwing loose earth over his shoulders. Some of it rolled back, but most of it remained up above. When the platform was full, he would have to climb up there and shovel the earth to the next platform. They were so deep now that the earth had to be handled four or five times before it was finally thrown out at the top. The hole was widening, too. The house would be undermined if some additional supports were not cut in the woods and drawn by the mules. He would have to send Black Sam and Uncle Felix with the mules to draw six or seven large logs the next morning.

Ty Ty did not know how long he had been digging when he heard Griselda calling him from the top of the ground.

"What's the matter, Griselda?" he asked, leaning wearily against the shovel.

"Where's that shotgun, Pa?" she asked. "Have you seen it?"

He waited a little while before answering her. He was too tired to speak until he had rested for a few moments.

"No, Griselda," he said finally. "I haven't seen it. I haven't got time to help you look for it now."

"Where in the world is it then, Pa? It was lying in the yard, and it's not there now."

"Griselda," he said, dropping his head so he would not have to look up at her, "Griselda, when Buck went for a walk, he carried it with him."

There was no sound above him on the rim of the crater, and presently he looked up to see if Griselda was still looking down at him. She was not within sight, but he distinctly heard the voices of Darling Jill and Rosamond raised in excitement somewhere up there on the top of the ground. He bent over his shovel, kicking the blade into the clay with his foot, and wondering how soon Shaw would come back to help him dig.

THE END